He'd told his bride very plainly that he never intended to love her. Love, he had said, was a destructive emotion. And perhaps that was what made him afraid now; he was afraid that his love would destroy Ana, would ruin their marriage.

His love was destructive.

"Vittorio…?" He felt Ana's hand on his sleeve, her voice no more than an uncertain whisper. She must have been standing there for some moments, waiting for him to notice her while he was lost in his reflections. Vittorio turned around.

"Good even—" He stopped, the words drying in his mouth, his head suddenly, completely empty of thoughts. The woman in front of him was stunning, a vision of ethereal loveliness in white lace. No, he realized distantly, she wasn't ethereal. She was earthy and real and so very beautiful. And she was his wife.

"You look amazing," he said, his voice low, heartfelt, and Ana smiled.

KATE HEWITT discovered her first Harlequin romance on a trip to England when she was thirteen, and she's continued to read them ever since. She wrote her first story at the age of five, simply because her older brother had written one and she thought she could do it, too. That story was one sentence long—fortunately, they've become a bit more detailed as she's grown older.

She studied drama in college, and shortly after graduation moved to New York City to pursue a career in theater. This was derailed by something far better—meeting the man of her dreams, who happened also to be her older brother's childhood friend. Ten days after their wedding they moved to England, where Kate worked a variety of different jobs—drama teacher, editorial assistant, youth worker, secretary and, finally, mother.

When her oldest daughter was one year old, she sold her first short story to a British magazine. Since then she has sold many stories and serials, but writing romance remains her first love—of course!

Besides writing, she enjoys reading, traveling and learning to knit—it's an ongoing process, and she's made a lot of scarves. After living in England for six years, she now resides in Connecticut with her husband, her three young children and the possibility of one day getting a dog.

Kate loves to hear from readers. You can contact her through her website, www.kate-hewitt.com.

THE MAN WHO COULD NEVER LOVE

KATE HEWITT

~ROYAL SECRETS ~

TORONTO NEW YORK LONDON
AMSTERDAM PARIS SYDNEY HAMBURG
STOCKHOLM ATHENS TOKYO MILAN MADRID
PRAGUE WARSAW BUDAPEST AUCKLAND

Recycling programs
for this product may
not exist in your area.

ISBN-13: 978-0-373-88181-9

THE MAN WHO COULD NEVER LOVE
Previously published in the U.K. as THE BRIDE'S AWAKENING

First North American Publication 2011

This edition published by arrangement with Harlequin Books S.A.

For questions and comments about the quality of this book
please contact us at Customer_eCare@Harlequin.ca.

® and TM are trademarks of the publisher. Trademarks indicated with
® are registered in the United States Patent and Trademark Office, the
Canadian Trade Marks Office and in other countries.

www.eHarlequin.com

Printed in U.S.A.

THE MAN WHO COULD NEVER LOVE

CHAPTER ONE

VITTORIO RALFINO, the Count of Cazlevara, stood on the threshold of San Stefano Castle and searched the milling guests for the woman he intended to be his wife. He wasn't certain what she looked like for, beyond a single small photo, he hadn't seen her in sixteen years. Or if he had seen her, she hadn't made much of an impression. Now he planned to marry her.

Anamaria Viale wasn't readily apparent amidst the tuxedo and evening gown-clad crowd circulating through the candlelit foyer. All he remembered from when he'd seen her at her mother's funeral was a sad, sallow face and too much dark hair. She'd been thirteen years old. The photo in the magazine gave little more information; she had good teeth. Still, her looks—or lack of them—did not interest Vittorio. Anamaria Viale possessed the qualities he was looking for in a wife: loyalty, health and a shared love of this land and its grapes. Her family's vineyard would be an asset to his own; together they would rule an empire and create a dynasty. Nothing else mattered.

Impatiently, he strode into the castle's medieval hall. Shadows danced along the stone walls and he felt the curious stares of neighbours, acquaintances and a few friends. He heard the murmur of speculative whispers travel around the ancient hall in a ripple of suppressed sound and knew he was their subject. He hadn't been back in Veneto for more than a day or two at a time in the last fifteen years. He'd kept away from the place and its memories and regrets. Like a hurt little boy, he'd run away from his past and pain, but he was a man now and he was home for good—to find a wife.

'Cazlevara!' Someone clapped him on the back, thrusting a glass of wine into his hand. His fingers closed around the fragile stem as a matter of instinct and he inhaled the spicy, fruity scent of a bold red. 'You must try this. It's Busato's new red—he's blended his grapes, *Vinifera* and *Molinara*. What do you think?'

Vittorio took a practised sip, swilling the rich liquid in his mouth for a moment before swallowing. 'Good enough,' he pronounced, not wanting to get into a detailed discussion about the merits of mixed grapes, or whether Busato, one of the region's smaller winemakers, was going to give Castle Cazlevara, his own winery—the region's largest and most select—any competition. He wanted to find Anamaria.

'I heard the rumours. You're home then? You're going to make some wine?'

Vittorio glanced at the man who had been speaking to him: Paolo Prefavera, a colleague of his father's. His round cheeks were already rosy with drink and he smiled with the genial bonhomie of an old family friend, although his eyes were shrewd.

'I've always been making wine, Paolo. Castle Cazlevara produces nine hundred thousand bottles a year.'

'While you've been touring the world—'

'It's called marketing.' Vittorio realized he was speaking through his teeth. He smiled. 'But yes, I'm home for good.' Home, so he could rein his grasping brother Bernardo back in, before he squandered the rest of the winery's profits. Home, so he could keep his treacherous mother from taking what was his—and his heir's. At this thought, his forced smile turned genuine, even though his eyes remained hard. 'Have you seen Anamaria Viale?' Paolo's eyebrows rose and Vittorio stifled a curse. He was too impatient; he knew that. When he made a decision, he wanted it carried out immediately, instantly. He'd decided to marry Anamaria Viale nearly a week ago; it felt like an eternity. He wanted it done; he wanted her vineyard joined to his, he wanted *her* joined to him, in his bed, by his side, being a wife.

Paolo smiled slyly and Vittorio forced himself to smile back. Now there would be whispers, rumours.

Gossip. 'I have a question to ask her,' he explained with a shrug, as if it were no matter.

'She was over by the fireplace, last time I saw her.' Paolo gave a small chuckle, more of a guffaw. 'How could you miss her?'

Vittorio didn't understand what Paolo meant until he neared the huge stone fireplace. An alarmingly large stuffed boar's head was mounted above the hearth and a few men were gathered underneath, sipping wine and chatting quietly. At least he thought they were all men. Narrowing his eyes, he realized the tall, strong figure in the centre of the group was actually a woman. Anamaria.

His mouth tightened as he took in his intended wife, dressed in an expensive-looking but essentially shapeless trouser suit. Her long dark hair was held back in a clip and looked as thick and coarse as a horse's tail. She held a glass of wine as most of the castle's guests did; the evening was, after all, a wine-tasting for the province's premier winemakers and guests. She had, Vittorio saw, strong, even features; pretty was not necessarily a word he would use to describe them. There was something too earthy and bold about her, he decided. He preferred the women he took to his bed to be more delicate, fragile even. *Slim*.

Not, he amended, that Anamaria Viale was overweight. Not at all. Big-boned was the word he might have chosen, although his mother would have sneered and called her *grassa*. Fat.

Vittorio's mouth thinned at the thought of his mother. He could hardly wait to see the look on the old bitch's face when he told her he was getting married. Bernardo, her precious favourite, fool that he was, would never inherit. Her plans—the plans she'd cherished since the moment his father's will had been read—would come to nothing.

Vittorio smiled at the thought, little more than a bitter twisting of his mouth, and dismissed his bride's looks as a matter of no importance. He didn't want a beautiful woman; beautiful women, like his mother and his last mistress, were never satisfied, always finding fault. He'd left his mistress in Rio pouting for more time, money, even love. He'd told her he would never set eyes on her again.

Anamaria, he was sure, would take what she was given and be grateful, which was exactly what he wanted. A wife—a humble, grateful wife—the most important accessory a man could ever possess.

Surveying her tall, strong form, Vittorio was quite sure a woman like her was unused to male attention; he anticipated her stammering, blushing pleasure when the Count of Cazlevara singled her out.

He stepped forward, straightening his shoulders, and adopted an easy-going, self-assured smile whose devastating effect he knew well.

'Anamaria.' His voice came out in a low, suggestive hum.

She turned, stiffening in surprise when she saw him. Her eyes widened and a smile dawned on her face, a fragile, tremulous gesture of joy, brightening her whole countenance for the barest of moments. Vittorio smiled back; he almost laughed aloud. This was going to be so easy.

Then she drew herself up—her height making Vittorio appreciate Paulo's comment once more—and raked him with one infuriatingly dismissive glance, that amazed smile turning cool and even—could it be?—contemptuous. He was still registering the change in her expression and mood—his smug satisfaction giving way to an uneasy alarm—when she spoke.

'Hello, Lord Cazlevara.' Her voice was low, husky. Almost, Vittorio thought with a flicker of distaste, like a man's. Although, he noted, there was nothing particularly unpleasing about her features: straight brows and nose, dark grey eyes, the good teeth he'd noticed before. She was not, at least, ugly; rather, she was exceedingly plain. He let his smile deepen to show the dimple in his cheek, de-termined to win this plain spinster over. A woman like Anamaria would surely appreciate any charm thrown her way.

'Let me be the first to say how lovely you look tonight.'

She raised her eyebrows, the flicker of that cool smile curling her mouth and glinting in her eyes. They had, he saw, gold flecks that made them seem to shimmer. 'You will indeed be the first to say so.'

It took Vittorio a moment to register the mockery;

he couldn't believe she was actually making fun of him—as well as of herself. Feeling slightly wrong-footed—and unused to it—Vittorio reached for her hand, intending to raise it to his lips even as he cursed the way he'd phrased his flattery. For flattery it was indeed, and she knew it. She was not stupid, which he supposed was a good thing. She let his lips brush her skin, something darkening her eyes—those gold flecks becoming molten—before she quite deliberately pulled her hand away.

The crowd around them had fallen back, yet Vittorio was conscious of avid stares, intent ears and, even more so, his own mounting annoyance. This first meeting was not going the way he'd anticipated—with him firmly in control.

'To what do I owe such a pleasure?' Anamaria asked. 'I don't believe we've seen each other in well over a decade.' Her voice caught a little, surprising him. He wondered what she was thinking of, or perhaps remembering.

'I'm simply glad to be back home,' Vittorio replied, keeping his voice pitched low and smooth, 'among beautiful women.'

She snorted. She actually snorted. Vittorio revised his opinion; the woman was not like a man, but a horse. 'You have learned honeyed words on your trips abroad,' she said shortly. 'They are far too sweet.' And, with a faintly mocking smile, she turned and walked away from him as if he were of no importance at all. *She* left *him*.

Vittorio stood there in soundless shock, his fury rising. He'd been summarily dismissed, and he, along with the little knot of spectators around him, was conscious of it. He felt the stares, saw a few smug smiles, and knew he'd been put properly in his place, as if he were a naughty schoolboy being disciplined by a mocking schoolmarm. It was a feeling he remembered from childhood, and he did not like it.

Standing there, Vittorio could not escape the glaringly—and embarrassingly—obvious conclusion: as far as opening gambits went, his had been an utter failure.

He'd been planning to ask her to marry him, if not tonight, then certainly in the next few days. When he decided a thing—even to marry—he wanted it done. Completed. Over. He had no time or patience for finer emotions, and frankly he'd considered the wooing of such a woman to be an easy exercise, a mere dispensing of charm, a few carefully chosen compliments.

After reading the article about her—and seeing her photo—he'd assumed she would be grateful for whatever attention she received. She was unmarried and nearing thirty; his proposal would be, he'd thought, a gift. Maybe even a miracle.

Perhaps he had been arrogant, or at least hasty. The wooing and winning of Anamaria Viale would take a little more thought.

Vittorio smiled. He liked challenges. Admittedly,

time was of the essence; he was thirty-seven and he needed a wife. An heir. Yet surely he had a week—or two—to entice Anamaria into marriage? He wasn't interested in making the woman fall in love with him, far from it. He simply wanted her to accept what was a very basic business proposition. She was the candidate he'd chosen, the most suitable one he could find, and he wasn't interested in any others. Anamaria Viale would be his.

Still, Vittorio realized, he'd acted like a fool. He was annoyed with himself for thinking a woman—any woman—could be charmed so thoughtlessly. It was a tactical error, and one he would not make again. The next time he met Anamaria Viale, she would smile at him because she couldn't help herself; she would hang on his every word. The next time he met her, it would be on his terms.

Anamaria made sure she didn't look back as she walked away from the Count of Cazlevara. Arrogant ass. Why on earth had he approached her? Although they were virtually neighbours, she hadn't seen him in at least a decade. He hadn't had more than two words for her in the handful of times she *had* seen him, and yet now he'd expressly sought her out at tonight's tasting, had looked for her and given her those ridiculous compliments.

Beautiful women. She was not one of them, and she knew it. She never would be. She'd been told enough. She was too tall, too big-boned, too mannish.

Her voice was too loud, her hands and feet too big; everything about her was awkward and unappealing to men like Vittorio, who had models and starlets and bored socialites on his arm. She'd seen the photos in the tabloids, although she pretended not to know. Not even to look. She did, on occasion anyway, because she was curious. And not just curious, but jealous, if she were honest with herself, which Anamaria always tried to be. She was jealous of those tiny, silly slips of women—women she'd gone to school with, women who had no use for her—who could wear the skimpy and sultry clothes she never could, who revelled in their own femininity while she plodded along, clumsy and cloddish. And Vittorio knew it. In the split second before she'd spoken, she'd seen the look in his eyes. Disdain, verging on disgust.

She knew that look; she'd seen it in Roberto's eyes when she'd tried to make him love her. Desire her. He hadn't. She'd seen it in other men's eyes as well; she was not what men thought of—or liked to think of—when they considered a woman. A pretty woman, a desirable one.

She'd become used to it, armoured herself with trouser suits and a practical, no-nonsense attitude, the best weapons a woman like her could have. Yet tonight, from Vittorio—stupidly—that look of disdain had hurt. She'd been so glad to see him, for that split second. Stupidly glad. She'd actually thought he'd remembered—

Why on earth had he approached her with that

asinine flattery? Had he been attempting some sort of misguided chivalry, or worse, had he been mocking her? And why had he sought her out so directly in the first place?

He was the Count of Cazlevara—he could have any woman he wanted—and yet he'd entered the party and made straight for her. She only knew that because she'd seen him enter the castle, and felt her heart skip and then completely turn over. Even from afar, he was magnificent; well over six feet, he walked with a lithe grace, his suit of navy silk worn with careless elegance. His eyes—as black as polished onyx—had narrowed and his assessing gaze had swept the hall as if he were looking for someone.

That was all she'd seen before she'd been pulled into another conversation, and now Anamaria wondered if he'd actually been looking for *her*.

Stupid. Fanciful. Wishful thinking, even. Vittorio could have anyone he wanted. Why on earth would he bother with her for a moment?

And yet, for some reason, he *had*.

Anamaria's cheeks burned and she took a hasty sip of wine, barely tasting the superb vintage—she was, ironically, drinking one of Cazlevara's own. It seemed, she acknowledged bleakly, far more likely that he'd been mocking her. Amusing himself with a little easy flattery of a woman who would surely only lap it up gratefully. She knew the type. She'd dealt before with men who treated her with condescending affection, and acted surprised when they were rebuffed. Yet Vittorio hadn't been surprised by her rebuff—he'd been furious.

Anamaria's lips curved into a smile. *Good.*

She knew very little about Vittorio. She knew the facts, of course. He was the richest man in Veneto, as well as a Count. His winery—the region's best—had been run by the Cazlevaras for hundreds of years. In comparison, her own family's three hundred year heritage seemed paltry.

His father had died when he was a teenager; she, along with several thousand others, had been at the memorial service at San Marco in Venice. The funeral had been a quiet family affair at the Cazlevara estate. As soon as he reached his majority, he'd gone travelling—drumming up more business for the winery—and hardly ever came home. He'd been more or less absent—gone—for nearly fifteen years. Anamaria could only imagine that a man like Vittorio needed more entertainment than the rolling hills and ancient vineyards Veneto could provide.

She pictured him now, remembering how he'd looked at her from those gleaming onyx eyes. He was a beautiful man, but in a hard way. Those high, sharp cheekbones seemed almost cruel—at least they did when his eyes were narrowed in such an assessing manner, his mouth pursed in telling disdain before he'd offered her such a false smile.

Yet, even as she considered how she'd seen him only a few moments ago, another memory rose up and swamped her senses. The only real memory she had of Vittorio Cazlevara. The memory that had made her smile when she'd seen him again—smile with hope and even, pathetically, with joy.

It had been at her mother's funeral. November, cold and wet. She'd been thirteen and hadn't grown into her body yet, all awkward angles, her limbs seeming to fly out of their own accord. She'd stood by the graveside, her hand smeared with the clump of muddy dirt she'd been asked to throw on her mother's casket. It had landed with a horrible thunk and she'd let out an inadvertent cry, the sound of a wounded animal.

As the mourners had filed out, Vittorio—he must have been around twenty years old then—had paused near her. It was only later that she'd wondered why he'd come at all; their families were acquaintances, nothing more. She hadn't registered the tall, dark presence for a moment; she'd been too shrouded in her own pall of grief. Then she'd looked up and those eyes—those beautiful eyes, dark with compassion—had met hers. He'd touched her cheek with his thumb, where a tear still sparkled.

'It's all right to be sad, *rondinella*,'—swallow—he'd said, softly enough so only she could hear. 'It's all right to cry.' She'd stared at him dumbly, his thumb still warm against her chilled cheek. He smiled, so sadly. 'But you know where your mother is now, don't you?' She shook her head, not wanting to hear some paltry platitude about how Emily Viale was happy now, watching her daughter from some celestial cloud. He took his thumb, damp with her tears, and touched it to his breastbone. 'In here. *Tua cuore.*' Your heart. And with another sad, fleeting smile, he had moved away.

She'd known then that he'd lost his father a few years before. Even so, she hadn't realized another person could understand her so perfectly. How someone—a stranger—had been able to say exactly the right thing. How later, when she wept scalding tears into her pillow, wept until she felt she'd be sick from it and her mind and body and heart all felt wrung, wasted, she'd remember his words.

It's all right to cry.

He'd helped her to grieve. And when the pain had, if not stopped, then at least lessened, she'd wanted to tell him that. She'd wanted to say thank you, and she supposed she'd wanted to see if he still understood her. Understood her more, even, than before. And she'd wanted to discover if she, perhaps, understood him too. A ridiculous notion, when that passing comment was the only conversation they'd ever really shared.

Over the years, she'd almost—almost—forgotten about Vittorio's words at her mother's graveside. Yet in that second when she'd seen him again, every frail, childish hope had leapt to life within her and she'd thought—she'd actually *believed*—that he remembered. That it had meant something.

Her pathetic foolishness, even if only for a second,

annoyed her. She wasn't romantic or a dreamer; any dreams of romance—love, even—she'd once entertained as a child had died out years ago, doused by the hard reality of boarding school, when she'd been a picked-on pigeon among swans. Ana's mouth twisted cynically. Perhaps not a pigeon, but a swallow, a plain and unprepossessing bird, after all.

They'd flickered briefly back to life in her university days, enough so that she had been willing to take a risk with Roberto.

That had been a mistake.

And, just now, the moment Vittorio Ralfino's mouth had tightened in disdain and then uttered words Anamaria knew to be false...the last faint, frail hope she hadn't even known she'd still possessed had flickered out completely. Mockery or lies. She didn't know which. It hardly mattered.

Anamaria took another sip of wine and turned to smile at another winemaker—Busato, a man in his sixties with hair like cotton wool and a smile as kind as that of *Babbo Natale*. As one of the few female winemakers in the room, she appreciated his kindness, as well as his respect. And, she told herself firmly, she would dismiss Vittorio Cazlevara completely from her mind, as he had undoubtedly dismissed her from his. A few words exchanged nearly seventeen years ago hardly mattered now. She wouldn't be surprised if Vittorio didn't remember them; it certainly shouldn't *hurt*. He'd merely been offering her a few pleasantries, scraps tossed from his opulent table, no doubt, and she vowed not to give them a second thought.

A light gleamed in one of the downstairs windows of Villa Rosso as she headed up the curving drive. Her father was waiting for her, as he always did when she went to these events; just a few years ago he would have gone with her, but now he chose to leave such things entirely to her. He claimed she needed her independence, but Anamaria suspected the socialising tired him. He was, by nature, a quiet and studious man.

'Ana?' His voice carried from the study as she entered the villa and slipped off her coat.

'Yes, Papà?'

'Tell me about the tasting. Was everyone there?'

'Everyone important,' she called back, entering the study with a smile, 'except you.'

'Bah, flattery.' Her father sat in a deep leather armchair by the fireplace; a fire crackled in the hearth to ward off the night's chill. A book lay forgotten in his lap and he took off his reading spectacles to look at her, his thin, lined face creasing into a smile. 'You needn't say such things to me.'

'I know,' she replied, sitting across from him and slipping off her shoes, 'and so I should, since I was the subject of a flatterer myself tonight.'

'Oh?' He shut his book and laid it on the side table, next to his spectacles. 'What do you mean?'

She hadn't meant to mention Vittorio. She'd

been trying to forget him, after all. Yet somehow he'd slipped right into their conversation before it had even started, and it couldn't even surprise her because, really, hadn't he been in her mind all evening?

'The Count of Cazlevara has returned,' she explained lightly. 'He made an appearance tonight. Did you know he was back?'

'Yes,' Enrico said after a moment and, to Ana's surprise, he sounded both thoughtful and guarded. 'I did.'

'Really?' She raised her eyebrows, tucking her feet under her as she settled deeper into the armchair of worn, butter-soft leather. 'You never told me.' She couldn't quite keep the faint note of reproach from her voice.

Her father hesitated and Ana had the distinct feeling he was hiding something from her. She wondered how she even knew it to be a possibility, when their relationship—especially in the years after her mother had died—had been so close, so open. It hadn't always been that way, God knew, but she'd worked at it and so had he, and yet now…? Was he actually hiding something from her?

She gave a little laugh. 'Well, Papà?'

He shrugged. 'It didn't seem important.'

Ana nodded, accepting, because of course it shouldn't be important. She barely knew Vittorio. That one moment by her mother's graveside shouldn't even count. 'Well, it's late,' she finally said, smiling. 'I'm tired, so I think I shall go to bed.'

Ana scooped up her shoes, letting them dangle from her fingers as she walked slowly from the library through the darkened foyer and up the marble stairs that led to the second floor of the villa. She walked past darkened room after darkened room; the villa had eight bedrooms and only two were ever used. They rarely had guests.

Vittorio's few words had unsettled her, she realized as she entered her room and began to undress for bed. They shouldn't have—what a meaningless conversation it had been! Barely two sentences, yet they reverberated through her mind, her body, their echoes whispering provocatively to her.

She hadn't expected to have such a reaction to the man when she'd barely spared him a thought these last years. Yet the moment he'd entered the castle, she'd been aware of him. Achingly, alarmingly, *agonizingly* aware, her body suddenly springing to life, as if it had been numb or asleep, or even dead.

She slipped on her pyjamas and let her hair out of its restraining clip.

Outside her window, the moon bathed the meadows in silver and she could just make out the shadowy silhouettes in the vineyard that gave Villa Rosso both its name and fortune—*rosso* for the colour of the wine those grapes produced, a rich velvety red that graced many a fine table in Italy and, more recently, abroad.

Ana sat in her window seat, her legs drawn up to her chest, her chin resting on her knees. The wind from the open window stirred her hair and cooled her cheeks—she hadn't realized they'd been heated. Had she been blushing?

And what for? If she had any sort of social life at all, that tiny exchange with Vittorio would have meant less than nothing. Yet the hard fact was that she didn't, and it had. She was twenty-nine years old, staring at her thirtieth birthday in just a few months, without even the breath of hope of a social life beyond the winemaking events and tastings she went to, mostly populated by men twice her age. Not exactly husband material.

And was she even looking for a husband? Ana asked herself sharply. She'd given up that kind of dream years ago, when it had been pathetically, painfully obvious that men were not interested in her. She'd chosen to fill her life with business, friends and family—her father, at least—rather than pursue romance—love—that had, over the years, always seemed to pass her by. She'd *let* it go by, knowing those things were not for her. She'd accepted it… until tonight.

Still, she wished now that Vittorio hadn't come back, wished his absurd flattery—false as it so obviously was—hadn't stirred up her soul, reminded her of secret longings she'd forgotten or repressed. She'd been ignored so long—as a woman—that she'd become invisible, even to herself. She simply didn't think of herself that way any more.

She leaned her head back against the cool stone, closing her eyes as the wind tangled her hair and rattled in the trees outside.

She wanted, she realized with a sharp pang, Vittorio Cazlevara to look at her not with disdain or disgust, but with desire. She wanted him to say the things he'd said to her tonight—and more—and mean them.

She wanted to feel like a woman. For once.

CHAPTER TWO

'SIGNORINA VIALE, YOU have a visitor.'

'I do?' Ana looked up from the vine she'd been inspecting. It was the beginning of the growing season and the vines were covered in tiny unripened fruit, the grapes like perfect, hard little pearls.

'Yes.' Edoardo, one of the office assistants, looked uncomfortable—not to mention incongruous—in his immaculate suit and leather loafers. He must have been annoyed at having to tramp out to the vineyard to find her, but Ana always seemed to forget to bring her mobile. 'It is Signor Ralfino…I mean the Count of Cazlevara.'

'Vittorio…?' Ana bit her lip as she saw Edoardo's surprised look. The name had slipped out before she could stop herself, yet she was hardly on intimate terms with the Count. Why was he here? It had been only three days since she'd last seen him at the wine-tasting event and now he'd come to Villa Rosso, to her home, to find her? She felt a strange prickling along her spine, a sense of ominous yet instinctive foreboding, the way she did before a storm. Even when the sun beat down from a cloudless sky, she could tell when rain was coming. She knew when to cover the grapes from frost. It was one of the things that made her a natural—and talented—winemaker. Yet she had no idea if her instincts were right when it came to men. She'd hardly had enough experience to find out. 'Is he in the office?' she asked, a bit abruptly, and Edoardo nodded.

The sun was hot on her bare head and Ana was suddenly conscious of her attire: dusty trousers and a shirt that stuck to her back. It was what she normally wore on her regular inspection of the Viale vineyards, yet she hardly expected to receive visitors in such clothing…and certainly not Vittorio.

Why was he here?

'Thank you, Edoardo. I'll be with him shortly.' Disconcerted by the sudden heavy thudding of her own heart, Ana turned back to the vines, stared blindly at the clusters of tiny grapes. She waited until she heard him leave, and the rustle of vines as he passed, and then she drew in a long shuddering breath. She unstuck her shirt from her back and brushed a few sweaty strands of hair from her forehead. She was a mess. This was not how she wanted the Count of Cazlevara to see her.

Unfortunately, she had no choice. She could hardly walk the half-kilometre back to the villa to change if Vittorio was already waiting in the winery office.

She'd undoubtedly kept him waiting long enough. Vittorio Cazlevara did not, Ana acknowledged, seem like a patient man. Taking another deep breath, she tried her best to straighten her clothes—how had her shirt become so untucked and with a long streak of dirt on one sleeve?—and, throwing back her shoulders, she headed towards the office.

The long, low building with its creamy stone and terracotta tiles was as much a home to Ana as the villa was. It was a place where she felt confident and in control, queen of her domain, and that knowledge gave her strength as she entered. Here, it didn't matter what she looked like or how she dressed. Here, she was Vittorio's equal.

Vittorio stood by the sofa that was meant for visitors, a coffee table scattered with glossy magazines in front of it. His hands shoved deep in his pockets, he prowled the small space with a restless energy that radiated from his powerful body. He looked like a caged panther, full of contained power, dark and vaguely threatening.

Yet why should she be threatened by him? He was just a man...but what a man. He wore an exquisite suit made of Italian silk, perfectly tailored and hugging his powerful frame—his tall frame, for he had at least four inches on her own five foot eleven. His hair was inky-dark and cut close, emphasizing those hooded onyx eyes, the slashes of his severe brows. He looked up and those knowing eyes fixed on her, making Ana realize she'd been gawping like a schoolgirl. She straightened, managing a small, cool smile.

'Count Cazlevara. An unexpected pleasure.'

'Vittorio, please.' His gaze swept her in an instant, his mouth tightening in what Ana recognized as that now familiar disdain. He didn't even realize how he gave himself away, she thought with a strange little pang of sorrow. Was he going to try some more asinine flattery on her? She braced herself, knowing, no matter what, it would hurt. 'I'm sorry if I've interrupted you,' Vittorio said, and Ana gestured to her dishevelled clothes, even managing a wry smile as if her attire was not humiliating, despite him being dressed with such exquisite care.

'I'm afraid I was not expecting visitors. I was out in the vineyard, as you can see.'

'How are your grapes?'

'Growing.' She turned away from him, surreptitiously tucking in her blouse, which seemed determined on coming untucked at every opportunity. 'The weather has been good, thank God. May I offer you refreshment?'

He paused, and she glanced back at him. His head was cocked, and he was studying her with a thoughtful thoroughness she decided she didn't like. 'Yes, thank you. It is a warm day.'

Did his eyes linger on her heated face, her sticky shirt? Ana willed herself not to flush even more. If even the Count of Cazlevara was going to arrive unannounced, he would have to take her as she was. 'Indeed. Why don't we adjourn to the tasting room? It is more comfortable in there.' Vittorio gave a terse little jerk of his head, and Ana led the way to the room at the back of the winery that was meant for public gatherings.

The room was light and airy, with a vaulted ceiling and large windows that let in the late morning sunshine. A few tables, made from retired oak barrels, were scattered around with high stools. Ana sat down on one of the leather sofas positioned in one corner, meant for a more intimate conversation. She sat down, smoothing her dusty trousers and offering Vittorio another smile, bright and impersonal. Safe. 'How may I help you, Vittorio?' She stumbled only slightly over his Christian name; she wasn't accustomed to using it, even if she had been thinking it to herself.

He didn't reply, instead giving her an answering smile that showed the white flash of his straight, even teeth and said, 'You've done well for yourself these last years, Anamaria. The Viale label has grown in stature—not to mention price.'

'Please call me Ana. And thank you. I've worked hard.'

'Indeed.' He steepled his fingers under his chin, surveying her with that knowing little smile that she now found irritated her. 'And you've stayed at Villa Rosso all these years?'

She gave a little shrug, trying not to be defensive. 'It is my home.'

'You haven't wanted to travel? Go to university? See a bit of the world?'

'I'm happy where I am, Vittorio,' Ana replied, her voice sharpening just a little bit. 'And I did go to university. I took a degree in viticulture at the University of Padua.'

'Of course.' He nodded. 'I forgot.' Ana almost asked him how he would have known such a thing in the first place, but she decided to hold her tongue. 'Your father must be very glad of your dedication and loyalty to Viale Wines—and to him, of course. You've lived with him all these years?'

'Yes.' Ana tilted her head, wondering where these seemingly innocuous comments were coming from. Why did the Count of Cazlevara care what she had been doing these last ten or fifteen years? What interest could he possibly have in Viale Wines? 'I cannot imagine doing anything else,' Ana said simply, for it was the truth. Viale Wines had become her life, her blood. Besides her father and her home, she had little else. Vittorio smiled, seeming pleased by her answer, and an assistant bustled in with a pitcher of iced lemon water and two frosted glasses.

'Thank you,' Ana murmured and, after the assistant had left, she poured two glasses and handed one to Vittorio. 'So,' she said when they'd both sipped silently for a moment, 'you're back at last from your travels abroad. To stay this time?'

'It would seem so. I have, I realize, been gone too long.' His mouth tightened, his eyes looking hard, and for a moment Ana was discomfited, wondering just what had brought him back to Veneto.

'Are you glad to be back?' she asked and his eyes, still hard with some unnamed emotion, met hers.

'Yes.'

Ana nodded. 'Still, it must have been nice to see so many places.' Could she sound more inane? She resisted the urge to wipe her damp palms on her trousers. She wanted to demand to know why he was here, what he wanted from her. This was the second time he'd sought her out, and she could not fathom why he was doing so. Why he would *want* to.

'It was.' He set his glass down on the coffee table with a quiet clink. 'And it was, of course, business.'

'Yes.'

Vittorio still gazed at her in that assessing manner, saying nothing. His silence unnerved her, made her edgy and a little desperate. She wasn't used to feeling so at odds; she'd become accustomed to being in control of her own life, especially here at the winery, her own little kingdom.

'Sometimes business and pleasure mix, however,' he finally said, his words seeming heavy with meaning, and Ana gave a little nod and smile although she hardly knew what he was saying, or why.

'Indeed.' Her nerves now taut and starting to fray, she forced another little laugh and said, 'I must confess, Vittorio, I don't know why you're here. It is good to have you back in Veneto, of course, but if I am to be frank, we've had very little to do with one another.' There. It was said. If she'd been rude, Ana

didn't care; his presence, so confident—arrogant—
and supremely male, unsettled her. It made her heart
jump and her palms sweat and, worst of all, it made
some sweet, nameless longing rise up in her like a
hungry tide. She swallowed and kept her gaze firmly
on him.

He leaned forward to take his glass once more,
and the scent of his cologne—something faintly
musky—wafted over her. Inadvertently, instinctively,
she pressed back against the sofa cushions. He lifted
his gaze to meet hers once more, yet she could tell
nothing from those onyx eyes. They were as blank
as polished marble. 'Actually, Ana, I came to ask
you to dinner.'

The words seemed to fall into the stillness of the
room, and of her heart. Did he mean a date? she
wondered incredulously, even as a sense of sudden
fierce pleasure rushed through her. A *date*. When
was the last time she'd been on one of those, and
with a man like Vittorio Ralfino? She felt her cheeks
heat—how easily she gave herself away—and to
cover her confusion, she reached for her glass and
took a sip.

'I see I've surprised you.'

'Yes.' She pressed the glass against her hot cheek,
lifting her gaze to smile wryly at him. 'We have
not seen each other in years and, in any case—'
She stopped, biting her lip, pulling it between her
teeth and nipping it hard enough to draw a drop of
blood. She tasted it on her tongue, hard and metallic.

Vittorio smiled, his eyes on her mouth, and Ana knew he'd witnessed that traitorous little display of her own uncertainty.

'In any case?' he prompted gently.

She gave a helpless little shrug. 'I'm not exactly the kind of woman—' She stopped again, wishing she had not revealed so much. She didn't know how *not* to; she was terrible at lying, or even dissembling. She could only speak her heart, always had. It had never been dangerous before.

And it had been so long—forever—since a man had asked her out. Since she'd even *hoped* a man might ask her out.

'The kind of woman I take out to dinner?' Vittorio filled in. 'But how would you know what kind of woman I take out to dinner?'

'I don't,' Ana said quickly, too quickly. 'But I know—' She stopped again. There was no way of saving herself or her pride, it seemed. 'I am surprised, that's all,' she finally said, and pressed her lips tightly together to keep from revealing anything more.

Vittorio didn't answer, and Ana couldn't tell a thing from his expression. Surprisingly, she found she was not blushing now; instead, she felt cold and lifeless. This—this feeling of terrible numbness—was why she'd stopped looking for a man, for love. It hurt too much.

She put her glass back down on the table. Memories rushed in to fill the blank spaces in her mind and heart. The cruel laughter of the girls at boarding school, the interminable school dances where she'd clutched a glass of lukewarm punch and tried to make herself invisible. It hadn't been hard to do; no one had wanted to see her anyway.

Stupid schoolgirl memories, yet how they still hurt. How another man's attention—and his disdain— brought it all back.

'I see,' he said finally and, on opening her eyes, Ana felt he saw too much. The last thing she wanted was his pity. 'Actually,' Vittorio continued, watching her carefully, 'I want to discuss a business proposition with you.' He waited, still watching, and Ana's eyes widened in horror. Now the blush came, firing her body from the roots of her hair to the tips of her toes. She'd made *such* a fool of herself, assuming he was asking her out. And of course he hadn't corrected her, she realized with a vicious little stab of fury. He'd probably enjoyed seeing her squirm, relished her awful confession. *I'm not exactly the kind of woman...* He knew just what she'd meant, and his expression told her he agreed with her. As many had before.

'A business proposition,' she finally repeated, the silence having gone on, awkwardly, for at least a minute. 'Of course.'

'It might not be the kind of business proposition you're expecting,' Vittorio warned with a little smile and Ana tried for an answering laugh, though inwardly she was still writhing with humiliation and remembered pain.

'Now you have me intrigued.'

'Good. Shall we say Friday evening?'

Ana jerked her head in acceptance. 'Very well.' It didn't seem important to pretend she needed to check some schedule, that she might be busy. That she might, in fact, have a *date*. Vittorio would see right through her. He already had.

'I'll pick you up at Villa Rosso.'

'I can meet you—'

'I am a gentleman, Ana,' Vittorio chided her wryly. 'I shall enjoy escorting you somewhere special.'

And where exactly was somewhere special? Ana wondered. And, more alarmingly, what should she wear? Her wardrobe of businesslike trouser suits hardly seemed appropriate for a dinner date...except it wasn't a date, had never been meant to be a date, she reminded herself fiercely. It was simply a business proposition. A trouser suit would have to do. Still, Ana was reluctant to don one. She didn't want to look like a man; she wanted to feel like a woman. She didn't dare ask herself why. For over ten years— since her university days—she'd dressed and acted not purposely like a man, more like a sexless woman. A woman who wasn't interested in fashion, or beauty, or even desire. Certainly not love. It had been safer that way; no expectations or hopes to have dashed, no one—especially herself—to disappoint. There was no earthly reason to change now. There was every reason to keep as she'd been, and stay safe.

On Friday night she stood in front of the full-length mirror in her bedroom, gazing rather ruefully at her reflection. She wore a pair of fitted black trousers with a rather unfortunately boxy jacket; it had looked better on the rack. Her one concession to femininity was the cream silk beaded tank top she wore underneath, and that was completely hidden by the jacket. She piled her hair up on top of her head, wincing a little bit at the strands that insisted on escaping to frame her face and curl with surprising docility along her neck. She couldn't decide if the loose tendrils gave her a look of elegance or dishevelment. She didn't attempt any make-up, as she'd never mastered the art of doing her face without looking like a child who had played in her mother's make-up box.

'There.' She nodded at her reflection, determined to accept what she saw. Wearing a sexy cocktail dress or elegant gown would have been ridiculous, she told herself. She never wore such things—she didn't own such things—and, considering Vittorio's business proposition, there was no reason to start now.

Her father was, as usual, in the study when Ana came downstairs. Most evenings he was content to hole up in the villa with a book or a game of solitaire.

Enrico looked up from his book, raising his eye-brows at her outfit. 'Going out, my dear?'

Ana nodded, suppressing a little pang of guilt. She hadn't told her father about this dinner with Vittorio; she told herself she'd simply forgotten, but she knew that wasn't true. She hadn't wanted him to know, and start reading more into this dinner than there was or ever could be.

'Yes,' she said now, dropping a kiss on the top of his thinning hair. 'Dinner.'

'A date?' Enrico asked, sounding pleased. Ana shook her head and stepped away to look out of the window. Twilight was stealing softly upon the world, cloaking the landscaped gardens in violet.

'No. Just business.'

'Always business,' her father said a bit grumpily, and Ana smiled.

'You know I love it.' And she did love it; the wine, the grapes were in her blood. Her father loved to tell the story about when he had taken her to the vine-yards when she was only two years old. He'd hoisted her up to the vines and she'd plucked a perfectly ripe grape, deeply purple and bursting with flavour, and popped it into her mouth. Then, instead of saying how tasty it was, she'd pronounced in a quite grown-up voice, *'Sono pronti.'* They're ready.

'I worry you work too much.'

Ana said nothing, for she knew she had no argu-ment. She did work too much; she had nothing else. In the last few years her father had stepped back from the winery business, as he'd never really wanted to be more than a gentleman vintner, tending the family grapes. Ana wanted more. She dreamed of the day when Viale wines were in every fine restaurant in Europe, and even America. When they were held in reserve for special customers, the bottles dusty and precious. When they rivalled Cazlevara Wines.

Just then she saw headlights pierce the growing darkness, and a navy Porsche swept up the drive. Ana watched from the window, her heart starting to thud with hard, heavy beats as Vittorio stepped from the car. In the lengthening shadows she couldn't see what he wore, yet she could tell he looked magnificent. She felt it in her own shivery response.

The doorbell rang.

'Someone is coming for you?' Enrico asked, his book forgotten in his lap.

'Yes—' Ana started from the study.

'Whoever it is,' Enrico called after her, 'invite him in.'

By the time she reached the door she was breathless and flushed, simply from nerves. Vittorio stood there, hands thrust deep into his pockets, looking as magnificent as Ana knew he would in an immaculately tailored suit of navy silk. His shirt was crisp and white and a tie of aquamarine silk was knotted at the brown column of his throat.

Ana swallowed, her mouth dry, her head empty of thoughts. She could not think of a single thing to say.

'Hello, Ana.' He smiled, a quick flash of white teeth. 'Are you ready?'

Ana nodded, conscious of both how Vittorio had not complimented her—or even commented on—her appearance, and that her father was sitting in the next room, waiting for her to usher in her guest. She swallowed. 'Yes, but would you like to come in for a moment? My father…' She trailed off, hating how hesitant she sounded. 'My father would like to say hello,' she said firmly, and then turned to lead Vittorio to the study without looking back to see if he followed.

Once in the study Ana stepped aside as her father looked up and smiled. He didn't, she realized with a jolt, look very surprised. 'Good evening, Vittorio.'

'Good evening, sir.'

Enrico smiled, pleased by the sign of respect. 'You are going out for dinner?'

'In a manner of speaking. I thought we could eat at Castle Cazlevara.'

Ana looked at him in surprise. Dinner in his own castle? She'd been to the castle once, for a Christmas party when she was a child. She remembered a huge Christmas tree, twenty feet high, in the castle's soaring entrance hall, and eating too many sweets.

Uneasily, Ana realized Vittorio and her father had been talking, and she hadn't heard a word. Now Vittorio turned to her, smiling solicitously. 'We should go.'

'Yes, all right.'

One hand rested lightly on the small of her back—the simple touch seemed to burn—as Vittorio said goodbye to Enrico and then led her out to the softly falling darkness and his waiting car.

Vittorio opened the passenger door for Ana before sliding in the driver's side. She was nervous, he saw, and her clothes were utterly atrocious. He'd been about to compliment her when she'd first opened the door and had just stopped himself from uttering what they both knew would be more unwanted false flattery.

He drummed his fingers against the steering wheel as Ana fastened her seat belt. He felt impatient, as he so often did, and also, strangely, a little uncertain. He didn't like either feeling. He didn't know how best to approach Ana, how to court her, if such a thing could even be done. He doubted he could act convincingly enough. As intelligent and decent a human being as she obviously was, she was not a woman to take to bed. Yet if this marriage was to work—if he were to have an heir—then he would be taking her to bed, and more than once.

Vittorio dwelt rather moodily on that scenario before pushing it aside. He could have chosen another woman, of course; there were plenty of pretty—gorgeous, even—socialites in Italy who would relish becoming the Contessa of Cazlevara. Women he would gladly take to bed but, ironically perhaps, he did not wish to marry them.

Their vineyards did not border his own; they were not dedicated to winemaking, to the region. They were not particularly loyal. They were not, any of them, wife material.

Ana was. When he'd contemplated taking a wife, Ana Viale had ticked every box quite neatly. Experienced in winemaking, running her own vineyard, a dutiful daughter, healthy and relatively young.

And, of course, loyalty. He'd read of her loyalty to her family, and her family's vineyard, in that magazine article. Loyalty was a necessity, an absolute; he would not be betrayed again, not by those closest to him.

No, Anamaria Viale was the wife he wanted. The only wife he wanted.

His hands tightened on the steering wheel as he thought of the other reason—really, the main reason—he wished to marry at all. He needed an heir. God willing, Ana would provide him with one, and would keep his brother—treacherous Bernardo—from ever becoming Count, as his mother had so recently told him she wanted.

The conversation, as it always was with Constantia, the current Countess, had been laced with bitterness on both sides. She'd rung asking for money; had there ever been anything else she wanted from him?

'I don't know why you hoard all your money, Vittorio,' she'd said a bit sulkily. 'Who are you keeping it for?'

He'd been distracted by the business emails on his computer screen, her words penetrating only after a moment. 'What do you mean?'

She'd sighed, the sound impatient and a bit contemptuous; it was a sound he remembered well from childhood, for it had punctuated nearly every conversation he'd had with his mother. 'Only that you are getting on in years, my son,' she had said, and he had heard the mocking note in her voice. 'You're thirty-seven. You are not likely to marry, are you?'

'I don't know,' he'd replied, and she'd laughed softly, the sound making the hair on the nape of his neck prickle.

'But if you don't marry, Vittorio, you can't produce an heir. And then you know what happens, don't you?' She sighed again, the sound different this time, almost sad. 'Bernardo becomes Count.'

He'd frozen then, his hand curled around the receiver, his eyes dark with memory and pain. That was what his mother had always wanted, what his brother had wanted. He'd known it for years, ever since they'd first tried to steal his inheritance from him, his father barely in the grave.

He didn't forget.

And how could he have forgotten the importance of marriage, of children? He'd been so intent on improving Cazlevara Wines, of forgetting the unhappiness he knew waited for him back home. He'd never considered the future, his future. His heirs.

Now he did. He'd considered carefully, chosen his

bride as he would a fine wine. Now he just needed to decide when to decant it.

Vittorio drummed his fingers against the steering wheel again and saw Ana slide him a wary glance. How to approach his chosen bride? She sat tensely, one hand clenched around the door handle as if she would escape the speeding car. The suit she wore looked like something pulled out of a convent's charity box and it did nothing for her tall, generous figure. Not that there was something to be done for her figure, but Vittorio imagined that some decent clothes and make-up could go some way to improving his intended bride's appearance.

His mouth twisted. What would Ana think if she knew he planned to marry her—and as soon as possible? Of course, any woman should be thrilled to become part of the Cazlevara dynasty, yet he felt instinctively that Ana Viale might balk. He knew from the other night at San Stefano Castle that she would not be fooled by his attempts to flatter or romance her, and why should she? God knew, the women he usually had on his arm or in his bed did not look or dress or even talk like Ana Viale. Yet he didn't want to marry them. He wanted to marry Ana. It was a matter of expediency, of business.

And that, Vittorio decided, was how he would present the marriage to her. She appreciated plain speaking, and so he would speak as plainly as possible. The thought appealed to him. He wouldn't have to waste time pretending to be attracted to her. Most women would enjoy a little flattery, but he knew now that it would only annoy Ana, perhaps even hurt her.

A tiny twinge of something close to guilt pierced his conscience. Would Ana want some kind of *real* marriage? Was she waiting for love?

With him it was impossible, and she needed to know that from the start. Surely a woman like her was not still holding out for love? She seemed too practical for that, not to mention too plain. Besides, she could always say no.

Except Vittorio would make sure she didn't.

Ana pressed back against the leather seat as the darkened countryside, rolling hills and clusters of oak trees, sped by. She sneaked another glance at Vittorio's rather forbidding profile. He hadn't spoken since they'd got in the car, and he didn't look as if he was up for a chat. His jaw was tight, his eyes narrowed, his hands clenched around the steering wheel. What was he thinking? Ana didn't want to ask. She turned towards the window, tried to still the nerves writhing in her middle. They drove for at least twenty minutes without speaking, and then Ana saw the lights of Castle Cazlevara on a hill in the distance, mere pinpricks in the unrelenting darkness. Vittorio turned into the mile-long private drive that wound its way up the hill to his home.

Ana had seen photos of the castle on postcards, and of course she'd been there the one time. Yet, even so, the sight of the huge medieval castle perched on jutting stone awed and even intimidated her. Its craggy turrets rose towards the darkened sky and an ancient-looking drawbridge was now lowered over the drained moat. At one point the castle had been an imposing fortress, perched high on its hill, surrounded by a deep moat. Now it was simply Vittorio's home.

'So your own home is the "somewhere special"?' she asked lightly, and was rewarded with the flicker of a smile.

'I must admit I find Castle Cazlevara rather special.'

Gazing up at the castle's soaring walls and towers, Ana could only agree. Special, and a bit scary.

Vittorio drove across the drawbridge and parked the car in the castle's inner courtyard, now paved over with slate, providing a perfect backdrop for the Porsche. The building had been updated from the time it had served as a fortress against barbarian invaders—and, if Ana remembered her history, the Pope's own army—although it still retained much of its charm. Though charm was hardly the word, Ana thought as Vittorio came around to open her door before she could even touch the handle. It was darkly impressive, forbiddingly beautiful. Like its owner. Gas-lit torches flickered on either side of the entrance doors as Vittorio led her up the stone stairs.

The huge entryway was filled with dancing

shadows, a thick Turkish carpet laid over the ancient stones. Polished mahogany doors led to several large reception rooms, now lost in shadow, but Vittorio forewent these in favour of a small passageway in the back of the main hall. Ana followed him, conscious of the castle all around them, huge, dark and silent.

'Have you ever wanted to build something else?' she asked to Vittorio's back. The narrow corridor was cold and dark. 'A palazzo somewhere, something modern?'

Vittorio stiffened slightly, yet noticeable still to Ana. She was so aware of him: his powerful shoulders and long back, the muscles rippling under the smooth silk of his suit, even the faint musk of him. Aware of his moods, changing like quicksilver, even though he did not look at her or speak. It was strange, being so aware. So *alive*. She wasn't used to it.

'The Counts of Cazlevara have always lived here,' he said simply. 'And their families. Although my mother lives near Milan for much of the year, in a palazzo like you mentioned.' There was a sharp note to his voice, a hint of something dark and even cruel, something Ana couldn't understand. He turned, his eyes gleaming from the light of the sconces positioned intermittently along the stone walls. 'Could you not imagine living in such a place as this?'

In a flash of insight—or perhaps just imagination—Ana *could* see herself living there. She pictured herself in the gracious drawing rooms, presiding over a Christmas party like the one she'd gone to as a child. Overseeing a feast in the ancient dining hall, as if she were the Contessa herself, inviting the citizens of Veneto into her gracious home. Such images caused longing to leap within her. Surprised by its intensity, she pushed the images away; they were absurd, impossible, and surely not what Vittorio meant.

'There is certainly a great deal of history here,' she said, once again to his back.

'Yes. Many centuries. Yet your own family has been in Veneto a long time.'

'Three hundred years,' Ana conceded wryly. 'No more than a day compared to yours.'

'A bit more than a day,' Vittorio said, laughter in his voice. He stopped in front of a polished wooden door which he opened so Ana could enter. 'And now. Dinner.'

Ana took in the cosy room with a mixture of alarm and anticipation. Heavy velvet curtains were drawn at the windows, blocking out the night. A fire crackled in the hearth and sent dancing shadows around the candlelit room. A table for two had been laid in front of the fire, with a rich linen tablecloth and napkins, the finest porcelain and crystal. On a small table to the side, a bottle of red had already been opened to breathe. It was an intimate scene, a romantic scene, a room ready not for business, but seduction.

Ana swallowed. She walked to the table, one hand

on the back of a chair. When had she last had a
meal like this, shared a meal like this? Never. The
idea of what was to come filled her with a dizzying
sense of excitement that she told herself she had no
right to feel. She shouldn't even want to feel it. Yet
still it came, bubbling up inside of her, treacherous
and hopeful. This felt like a date. A real date. She
cleared her throat. 'This all looks lovely, Vittorio.
Somewhere special indeed.'

Vittorio smiled and closed the door behind him.
They were completely alone; Ana wondered whether
there was anyone else in the castle at all. 'Do you
live here alone since you've returned?' she asked.

Vittorio shrugged. 'My brother Bernardo and my
mother Constantia are in Milan. They come and go
as they please.'

His tone was strange, cold, and yet also almost
indifferent. It made Ana wonder if he considered his
brother and mother—the only family he had left—as
nothing more than interlopers in his own existence.
Surely not. Ever since her own mother had died,
she'd clung to her father, to the knowledge that he
was her closest and only relative, that all they had
was each other. Surely Vittorio felt the same?

He pulled back her chair and Ana sat, suppressing a shiver of awareness as he took the heavy linen
napkin and spread it across her lap, his thumbs
actually brushing her inner thighs. Ana jerked in
response to the touch, a flush heating her cheeks,
warming her insides. She had never been touched so

intimately, and the thought was shaming. He'd just been putting a napkin in her lap.

She supposed it was her lack of experience with men that made her so skittish and uncertain around Vittorio, hyper-aware of everything he did, every sense stirring to life just by being near him. That had to be it; nothing else made sense. This aching awareness of him was just due to her own inexperience. She didn't go on dates and she didn't flirt. She did not know what it felt like to be desired.

And you're not desired now.

This dinner—this room—with all of its seeming expectations was going to her head. It was setting her up, Ana realized, for a huge and humiliating fall. She'd fallen before, she reminded herself, her would-be boyfriend at university had had to spell out the plain truth.

I'm just not attracted to you.

Neither was Vittorio. He wasn't even pretending otherwise. She mustn't forget that, no matter what the trappings now, Vittorio was not interested in her as a woman. This was simply how he did business. It had to be.

And so it would be how she did business as well.

'Wine?' Vittorio asked and held up the bottle. With a little dart of surprised pleasure, Ana realized it was one of Viale's labels. The best, she acknowledged as she nodded and Vittorio poured.

He sat down across from her and raised his glass.

Ana raised her own in response. 'To business propositions.'

'Intriguing ones, even,' Ana murmured, and they both drank.

'Delicious,' Vittorio pronounced, and Ana smiled.

'It's a new blend—'

'Yes, I read about it.'

She nearly spluttered in surprise. 'You did?'

'Yes, in the in-flight magazine on my trip home.' Vittorio placed his glass on the table. 'There was a little article about you. Have you seen it?' Ana nodded jerkily. The interview had been short, but she'd been glad—and proud—of the publicity. 'You've done well for yourself, Ana, and for Viale Wines.'

'Thank you.' His words meant more to her than they ought, she knew, but she couldn't keep the fierce pleasure at his praise from firing through her. Ana had worked long and hard to be accepted in the winemaking community, to make Viale Wines the name it was.

A few minutes later a young woman, diminutive and dark-haired, came in with two plates. She set them down, Vittorio murmured his thanks and then she left as quietly as she had come.

Ana glanced down at the paper-thin slices of prosciutto and melon. 'This looks delicious.'

'I'm glad you think so.'

They ate in silence and Ana's nerves grew more and more taut, fraying, ready to break. She wanted to demand answers of Vittorio; she wanted to know just what this business proposition was. She wasn't good at this, had never been good at this; she couldn't banter or flirt, and at the moment even idle chatter seemed beyond her.

It was too much, she thought with a pang. Being here with a devastatingly handsome man—with Vittorio—eating delicious food, drinking wonderful wine, watching the firelight play with shadows on his face—all of it was too much. It made her remember all the things she'd once wanted that she'd long ago accepted she'd never have. A husband. Children. A home of her own. She'd made peace with that, with the lack in her life, because there was so much she had, so much she loved and enjoyed. She'd *thought* she'd made peace with it, but now she felt restless and uncertain and a little bit afraid. She *wanted* again.

She had no idea why Vittorio—Vittorio, of all people, who was so unbearably out of her league—made her feel this way. Made her remember and long for those things. Made her, even now, wonder if his hair felt as crisp as it looked, or if it would be soft in her hands. If she touched his cheek would she feel the flick of stubble against her fingers? Would his lips be soft? Would he taste like her own wine?

Ana nearly choked on a piece of melon, and Vittorio looked up enquiringly. 'Are you all right?' he asked, all solicitude, and she nodded almost frantically.

'Yes—yes, fine.' She could hardly believe the direction her thoughts had taken, or the effect they were having on her body. Her limbs felt heavy and warm, a deep, pleasurable tingling starting low in her belly and then suddenly, mischievously flaring upwards, making her whole being clench with sudden, unexpected spasms of desire.

She'd never thought to feel this way, had thought—hoped, even—she'd buried such desperate longings. For surely they were desperate. This was *Vittorio*. Vittorio Ralfino, the Count of Cazlevara, and he'd never once looked at her as a woman. He never would.

They ate in near silence, and when they were finished the woman came back to clear the plates and replace them with dishes of homemade ravioli filled with fresh, succulent lobster.

'Have you missed home?' Ana asked in an effort to break the strained silence. Or perhaps it wasn't strained and she only felt it was because her nerves were so fraught, her body still weak with this new desire, desperate for more. Or less. She was torn between the safety of its receding and the need for it to increase. To actually touch. Feel. *Know*.

Vittorio seemed utterly unaware of her dilemma; he sat sprawled in his chair, cradling his glass of wine between his palms.

'Yes,' he replied, taking a sip. 'I shouldn't have stayed away so long.'

Ana was surprised by the regret in his voice. 'Why did you?'

He shrugged. 'It seemed the right thing to do at the time. Or, at least, the easy thing to do.' Vittorio took a bite of ravioli. 'Eat up. These ravioli are made right here at the castle, and the lobster were caught fresh only this morning.'

'Impressive,' Ana murmured, and indeed it was delicious, although she barely enjoyed a mouthful for she felt the tension and the need building inside her, tightening her chest and making it hard even to breathe. She wanted to ask him what she was doing here; she wanted to reach across the table and touch him. The need to touch was fast overriding the need to know. Action would replace words and if she had just one more glass of wine she was afraid she would do just what she was thinking—fantasising—about and actually touch him.

She wondered how Vittorio would react. Would he be stunned? Flattered? Repulsed? It was too dangerous to even imagine a scenario, much less to want it—crave it…

She could stand it no more. She set down her fork and gave Vittorio as direct a look as she could. 'As lovely as this meal is, Vittorio, I feel I have to ask. I must know.' She took a breath and let it out slowly, laying her hand flat on the table so she didn't betray herself and reach out to touch him. 'Just what is this business proposition you are thinking of?'

Vittorio didn't answer for a long moment. He

glanced at the wine in his glass, ruby-red, glinting in the candlelight. He smiled almost lazily—making her insides flare with need once more—and then set his glass down on the table.

'Well,' he said with a wry little smile, 'if you must know, it is simply this. I want you to marry me.'

CHAPTER THREE

THE words seemed to ring in the empty air, filling the room, even though the only sound was the crackle of the fire as the logs settled into the grate, scattering a bit of ash across the carpet.

Ana stared, her mind spinning, her mouth dry. Once again, she couldn't think of a single thing to say. She wondered if she'd heard him correctly. Surely she'd imagined the words. Had she wanted him to say such a thing? Was she so ridiculous, pathetic, that she'd *dreamed* it?

Or had he been joking? Common sense returned. Of course he was joking. She let her lips curve into a little smile, although she knew the silence had gone on too long. She reached for her wine. 'Really, Vittorio,' she said, shaking her head a little bit as if she actually shared the joke, 'I want to know why.'

He leaned forward, all lazy languor gone, replaced with a sudden intentness. 'I'm serious, Ana. I want to marry you.'

She shook her head again, unable to believe it.

Afraid to believe it. He must be joking, even if it was a terrible joke. A cruel one.

She'd known cruel jokes before. Girls hiding her clothes after gym, so she had to walk through the locker rooms in a scrap of a towel while they giggled and whispered behind their hands. The boy who had asked her to dance when she was fifteen—she'd accepted, incredulously, and he'd laughed and run away. She'd seen the money exchange grubby adolescent hands, and realized he'd only asked her as a bet. And of course the one man she'd let into her life, had wanted to give her body to, only to be told he didn't think of her that way. Roberto had acted affronted, as if she'd misunderstood all the time they'd spent together, the dinners and the late nights studying. Perhaps she had misunderstood; perhaps she was misunderstanding now.

Yet, looking at Vittorio's calm face, his eyes focused intently on hers, Ana slowly realized she hadn't misunderstood. He wasn't joking. He was serious. And yet surely he couldn't be—surely he could not possibly want to marry *her*.

'I told you the proposition was an intriguing one,' he said, and there was laughter in his voice.

'That's one word for it,' Ana managed, and took a healthy draught of wine. It went down the wrong way and for a few seconds her eyes watered as she tried to suppress a most inelegant cough. A smile lurked in Vittorio's eyes, in the upward flick of his mouth and he reached out to touch her shoulder, his hand warm even through the thick cloth of her jacket.

'Just cough, Ana. Better out than in.'

She covered her mouth with her hand, managing a few ladylike coughs before her body took over and she choked and spluttered for several minutes, tears streaming from her eyes, utterly inelegant. Vittorio poured her a glass of water and thrust it into her hands.

'I'm sorry,' she finally managed when she had control over herself once more. She wiped her eyes and took a sip of water.

'Are you all right?' She nodded, and he leaned back in his chair. 'I see I've surprised you.'

'You could say that.' Ana shook her head, still unable to believe Vittorio had actually said what she'd thought he had said. And if he had said it, why? What on earth was he thinking of? None of it made sense. She couldn't even *think*.

'I didn't intend to speak so plainly, so quickly,' Vittorio said, 'but I thought you'd appreciate an honest business proposition.'

Ana blinked, then blinked again. She glanced around the room with its flickering candles and half-drunk glasses of wine, the fire burned down to a few glowing embers; the desire still coiled up inside her, desperate to unfurl. What a fool she was. 'Ah,' she said slowly, 'business.' Marriage must, for a man like Vittorio, determined and ambitious, be a matter of business. 'Of course.' She heard the note of disappointment in her own voice and cringed inside. Why should she feel let down? Everything she'd wanted and felt—that had been in her own head. Her own body. Not Vittorio's. She turned to gaze at him once more, her expression direct and a little flat. 'So just how is marriage a business proposition?'

Vittorio felt the natural vibrancy drain from Ana's body, leaving the room just a little bit colder. Flatter. He'd made a mistake, he realized. Several mistakes. He'd gone about it all wrong, and he'd tried so hard not to. He'd seen her look around the room, watched her take in all the trappings of a romantic evening which he'd laid so carefully. The fire, the wine, the glinting crystal. The intimate atmosphere that wrapped around them so suggestively. It was not, he realized, a setting for business. *Fool.* If he'd been intending to conduct this marriage proposal with a no-nonsense business approach, he should have done it properly, in a proper business setting. Not here, not like this. This room, this meal promised things and feelings he had no intention or desire to give. And Ana knew it. That was why she looked so flat now, so…*disappointed.*

Did she actually want—or even expect—that from him? Had she convinced herself this was a *date*? The thought filled Vittorio with both shame and disgust. He could not, he knew, pretend to be attracted to her. He shouldn't even try. He shouldn't have brought her to this room at all. He needed to stop pretending he was wooing her. Even when he knew he wasn't, he still fell back on old tactics, old ploys that had given him success in the past.

Now was the time for something new.

Vittorio leaned forward. 'Tell me, Ana, do you play cards?'

Ana looked up, arching her eyebrows in surprise. 'Cards…?'

'Yes, cards.' Vittorio smiled easily. 'I thought after dinner we could have a friendly game of cards—and discuss this business proposition.'

She arched her eyebrows higher. 'Are you intending to wager?'

Vittorio shrugged. 'Most business is discussed over some time of sport or leisure—whether it is golf, cards, or something else entirely.'

'How about billiards?'

Vittorio's own eyebrows rose, and Ana felt a fierce little dart of pleasure at his obvious surprise. 'You play billiards?'

'*Stecca*, yes.'

'*Stecca*,' Vittorio repeated. 'As a matter of fact, the castle has a five pins table. My father put it in when he became Count.' He paused. 'I played with him when I was a boy.'

Ana didn't know if she was imagining the brief look of sorrow that flashed across Vittorio's face. She remembered hearing, vaguely, that he'd been very close to his father.

It's all right to be sad, rondinella.

She pushed the memory away and smiled now with bright determination. 'Good. Then you know how to play.'

Vittorio chuckled. 'Yes, I do. And I have to warn you, I'm quite good.'

Ana met his dark gaze with a steely one of her own. 'So am I.'

He led her from the cosy little room with the discarded remains of their meal, down another narrow corridor into the stone heart of the castle and then out again, until he came to a large, airy room in a more recent addition to the castle, with long sash windows that looked out onto a darkened expanse of formal gardens. In the twilit shadows Ana could only just discern the bulky shapes of box hedges and marble fountains. The room looked as if it hadn't been used in years; the billiards table was covered in dust sheets and the air smelled musty.

'I suppose you haven't played in a while,' she said, and Vittorio flashed a quick grin that once more caused her insides to fizz and flare. She did her best to ignore the dizzying sensation, pleasant as it was.

'Not here, anyway.' He pulled the sheet off the table and balled it up, tossing it in a corner, then opened the windows so the fresh, fragrant air wafted in from the gardens. 'The cues are over there. Do you want something to drink?'

Ana felt reckless and a little bit dangerous; she

knew why Vittorio had asked her if she played cards, why they were here about to play billiards instead of back in that candlelit room. This was business. *She* was business. He could not have made it plainer. And that was fine; she could handle this. Any disappointment she'd felt—unreasonably so—gave way to a cool determination. 'I'll have a whisky.'

Vittorio gazed at her for a moment, his expression thoughtful and perhaps even pleased, his mouth curling upwards into a little smile before he nodded and went to push a button hidden discreetly by the door. Within minutes another servant—this time a man, some kind of butler—appeared at the doorway, silent and waiting.

'Mario, two whiskies please.'

'Yes, my lord.'

Ana selected her cue and carefully chalked the end. She studied the table with its three balls: two cue balls, one white, one yellow and a red object ball. Vittorio was setting up the castle in the middle of the table: five skittles, four white, one red, made into a cross. The object of the game was simple: you wanted to knock your opponent's ball into the skittles for points, or have it hit the red object ball. Her father liked to say it was a grown-up game of marbles.

'So where did you learn to play *stecca*?' Vittorio asked as he stepped back from the table.

'My father. After my mother died, it was a way for us to spend time together.'

'How touching,' he murmured, and Ana knew he meant it. He sounded almost sad.

'And I suppose your father taught you?' she asked. 'Or did you play with your brother?' She leaned over the table and practised a shot, the cue stick smooth and supple under her hands.

'Just my father.'

Ana stepped back, letting the cue stick rest on the floor. 'Would you like to go first?'

Vittorio widened his eyes in mock horror. 'Would a gentleman ever go first? I think not!'

Ana gave a little laugh and shrugged. 'I just wanted to give you the advantage. I warned you I was good.'

Vittorio threw his head back and let out a loud laugh; the sight of the long brown column of his throat, the muscles working, made something plunge deep inside Ana and then flare up again in need. Suddenly her hands were slippery on the cue stick and her mouth was dry. She was conscious of the way her heart had started beating with slow, deliberate thuds that seemed to rock her whole body. 'And I told you I was good too, as I remember.'

'Then we'll just have to see who is better,' Ana returned pertly, smiling a little bit as if she was relaxed, as if her body wasn't thrumming like a violin Vittorio had just played with a few words and a laugh.

The servant entered quietly with a tray carrying two tumblers, a bottle of Pellegrino and another

bottle of very good, very old single malt whisky.
Ana swallowed dryly. She'd only said she wanted
whisky because she'd known what Vittorio was
up to; she'd felt reckless and defiant and whisky
seemed like the kind of drink men drank when they
were playing a business games of billiards.

She, however, didn't drink it. She had a few sips
with her father every now and then, but the thought
of taking a whole tumbler with Vittorio made her
nervous. She was a notorious lightweight—especially for a winemaker—and she didn't want to
make a fool of herself in front of him. Especially
not with this desire—so treacherous, so overwhelming, so new—still warring within her, making her
feel languorous and anxious at varying turns.

'So,' Vittorio said as he reached for the whisky,
'do you take yours neat or with a little water?'

Water sounded like a good idea, a way to weaken
the alcohol. 'Pellegrino, please.'

'As you wish.' He took his neat, Ana saw, accepting her tumbler with numb fingers. Vittorio
smiled and raised his glass and she did likewise.
They both sipped, and Ana managed not to choke
as the whisky—barely diluted by water—burned
down her throat.

'Now, please,' Vittorio said, sweeping his arm in
an elegant arc. 'Ladies first.'

Ana nodded and set her glass aside. She lined up
her first shot, leaning over the table, nervous and shy
as Vittorio watched blandly. Focus, she told herself.

Focus on the game, focus on the business. Yet that thought—and its following one, *marriage*—made her hands turn shaky and the shot went wide.

Vittorio clicked his tongue. 'Pity.'

He was teasing her, Ana knew, but she ground her teeth anyway. She hated to lose. It was one of the reasons she was so good at *stecca*; she'd spent hours practising so she could best her father at the game, which she hadn't done until she was fifteen. It had been five years of practice and waiting.

She stepped back from the table and took another sip of whisky as Vittorio lined up his shot. 'So why *do* you want to marry me?' she asked, her tone one of casual interest, just as he prepared to shoot. His shot went as wide as her own.

He swung around to face her, his eyes narrowed, and Ana smiled sweetly. 'I think you'd make an appropriate wife.'

'Appropriate. What a romantic word.'

'As I said,' Vittorio said softly, 'this is a matter of business.'

Ana lined up her own shot; before Vittorio could say anything else, she took it, banking his ball and missing the skittle by a centimetre. She'd been a fool to mention romance. 'Indeed. And you see marriage as a matter of business?'

He paused. 'Yes.'

'And what about me is so appropriate?' Ana asked. 'Out of curiosity.' Vittorio took his shot and knocked her ball cleanly into a skittle. Ana stifled a curse.

'Everything.'

She let out an incredulous laugh. 'Really, Vittorio, I am not such a paragon.'

'You are from a well-known, respected family in this region, you have worked hard at your own winery business these last ten years, and you are loyal.'

'And that is what you are looking for in a wife?' Ana asked, her tone sharpening. 'That is quite a list. Did you draw it up yourself?' She took another shot, grateful that this time she knocked his ball into a skittle. They were even, at least in billiards.

Vittorio hesitated for only a fraction of a second. 'I know what I want.'

She had to ask it; she had to know. She kept her voice light, even dismissive. 'You are not interested in love, I suppose?'

'No.' He paused. 'Are you?'

Ana watched as he stilled, his head cocked to one side, his dark eyes narrowed and intent as he waited for her answer. What a strange question, she thought distantly. Weren't most people interested in love?

Yet, even as she asked the question, she knew the answer for herself. She was not—could not—be interested in love, the love of a man, romantic, sexual. She'd tried it once and had felt only failure and shame—both feelings had taken years to forget, and even now she remembered the way they'd roiled through her, Roberto's horrified look...

No. Love—that kind of love—Ana had long ago

accepted, was a luxury she could neither afford nor access. Yet did she want it? Crave it? *Need* it? Ana knew the answer to that question as well. No, she did not. The risk was simply too great, and the possibility—the hope—too small. 'No,' she said coolly. She leaned over for her next shot, determined to focus completely on the game. 'I'm not.'

'Good.'

She took the shot and straightened. 'I thought you'd say that.'

'It makes it so much easier.'

'Easier?' she repeated, and heard the sardonic note in her voice. When had she become so cynical? From the moment Vittorio had proposed a marriage of convenience, or before? Long before?

'Some women,' Vittorio said carefully, 'would not accept the idea of a marriage based on common principles—'

'Based on business, you mean.'

'Yes,' Vittorio said after a moment, 'but you must realize that I mean this to be a true marriage.' He paused. 'A *proper* marriage, a marriage in every sense of the word.'

Naïve virgin she may be, but Ana still knew what Vittorio was talking about. She could imagine it all too easily. Or almost. She closed her eyes briefly, but if she wanted to banish the image, she failed. It came back clearly, emblazoned on her brain. An antique four-poster, piled high with pillows and cushions. Vittorio, naked, tangled in sheets. Magnificent. Hers.

Ana turned back to the billiards table. 'So,' she said, blindly lining up a shot, 'you mean sex.' She didn't—couldn't—look at him, even as she kept her voice nonchalant. She missed her shot entirely.

'Yes.' Vittorio sounded completely unmoved. 'I'd like children. Heirs.'

'Is that really why you're marrying?'

He hesitated for only a second. 'The main reason,' he allowed and Ana felt a ripple of disappointment, although she hardly knew why. Of course a man like Vittorio wanted children, would marry for an heir. Heirs. He was a count; he had a title, a castle, a business, all to pass on to his child. A hoped-for son, no doubt. Her son. The thought sliced through her, shocking her, not an altogether unpleasant feeling. Vittorio arched his brows. 'Do you want children, Ana?'

There was something intimate about the question, especially when he spoke in that low, husky tone that made her insides ripple and her toes curl. She'd never expected to have such a fierce, primal reaction to him. It was instinctive and sensual, and it scared her. She turned away.

'Yes, I suppose.'

'You only suppose?'

'I never thought to have children,' she admitted with a bleak honesty that turned her voice a bit ragged. 'I never thought to have the opportunity.'

'Then this marriage suits us both.'

She gave a little instinctive shake of her head. He

spoke as if it were agreed, the proverbial done deal. It couldn't be that easy. *She* couldn't be that easy.

'No.'

'Why not?' He'd moved closer to her; she could feel him by her shoulder, the heat and the musk of him.

'We're talking about marriage, Vittorio. A lifetime commitment.'

'So?'

'Such a decision requires some thought.'

'I can assure you I have thought of it a good deal.'

'Well, I haven't.' She turned around, suddenly angry. 'I haven't thought about it at *all*.'

He nodded, annoyingly unperturbed. 'You must have questions.'

She didn't answer. Of course she had questions, but they weren't ones she necessarily wanted to ask. *Why do you want to marry me? What if we hate each other? Do you even desire me at all?*

Why am I so tempted?

She looked up, taking a breath. 'I don't even know what you think of marriage…of a wife. What would you expect of me? How would we…get on…together?' It seemed ridiculous even to ask the questions, for surely she wasn't seriously considering his outrageous proposal. Yet, even so, Ana was curious. She wanted to know the answers.

'We'd get on together quite well, I imagine,' Vittorio replied easily. Ana wanted to scream.

You're not attracted to me, she wanted to shout. *I saw how you looked at me in that first moment— you summed me up and dismissed me! And now you want to marry me?*

She'd convinced herself she could live without love. But desire? Attraction? Could she give her body to a man who looked at her with disdain or, worse, disgust? Could she live with herself, if she did that, day after day?

'Ana, what are you thinking?' Vittorio's voice was gentle, concerned. She almost wanted to tell him, yet she knew she couldn't bear the truth of his confession, or the deception of his denial. She let out a long shuddering breath.

'Surely there are other women who fulfil your criteria,' she said at last.

Vittorio shook his head. 'No. There are few women with your knowledge of wine, Ana, or of this region. And of course your vineyard combined with mine would give us both a legacy for our children. And I appreciate your breeding and class—'

'You make me sound like a horse. I'm as good as, aren't I?' Calm once more, she spoke without rancour, merely stating the rather glum fact.

'Then consider me one as well.'

'A stallion, you mean?' and her mouth quirked upwards with wry amusement in spite of all the hurt and disappointment she felt.

'Of course.' Vittorio matched her smile. 'If I am considering this marriage a business, there is no reason you cannot as well. We are each other's mutual assets.'

Ana bit her lip. He made it sound so easy, so obvious. So natural, as if bartering a marriage over billiards in this day and age was a perfectly normal and acceptable thing to do. Vittorio had already told her he would not love her. Yet, Ana asked herself with bleak honesty, would someone else, *if* she were interested in love, which she'd already told herself she wasn't? Funny how much convincing that took.

She would be thirty years old in just two months. She hadn't had a date of any kind in over five years, and the last one had been appalling, an awkward few hours with a man with whom she'd shared not one point of sympathy. She'd never had a serious boyfriend. She'd never had *sex*. Was Vittorio's offer the best she'd get?

And, Ana acknowledged as she sneaked a glance at him from under her lashes, she could certainly do worse. He'd shed his jacket and tie and undone the top two buttons of his shirt. Under the smooth luxurious fabric, his muscles moved in sinuous elegance. His dark hair gleamed in the dimly lit room like polished ebony. The harsh lines of his jaw and cheek were starkly beautiful… He was beautiful. And he wanted to be her husband.

The thought was incredible. Insane. It couldn't work. It wouldn't. Vittorio would come to his senses, Ana would feel that devastating disappointment once again.

He wouldn't desire her. She'd see it in his eyes, feel it in his body—

And yet. Yet. Even now, she considered it. Even now, her mind raced to find possibilities, solutions. *Hope*. Some part of her wanted to marry Vittorio. Some part of her wanted that life. That, Ana knew, was why she hadn't dismissed him immediately and utterly. It was why she was asking questions, voicing objections as if this absurd and insulting proposal had any merit. Because, to some small suppressed part of her soul, it *did*.

Ana stood up and reached for her cue stick. 'Let's play,' she said, her voice brusque. She didn't want to talk any more. She didn't want to think about any of it. She just wanted to beat the hell out of the Count of Cazlevara.

Vittorio watched as Ana shrugged off her boxy jacket, tossing it onto a chair. She glanced over her shoulder, her eyes dark and smoky with challenge. 'Ready?'

Vittorio felt his insides tighten with a sudden surprising coil of desire. One sharp dart of lust. Without that awful jacket, he could actually see some of Ana's body. She wore a hugging top of creamy beaded silk that pulled taut over her generous breasts as she leaned forward to line up her shot. Vittorio found his gaze fixed first on the back of her neck, where a long tendril of dark hair lay curled against her skin. Her hair wasn't brown, he realized absently, it was myriad colours. Brown and black and red and even gold. His gaze dropped instinctively lower, to her backside. Bent over the billiards table, the fabric of her trousers pulled tightly across her bottom. The realization caused another shaft of lust to slice through him and he found he was gripping his cue stick rather tightly. He'd thought she had a mannish figure because she was tall. Yet, seeing her now, her curves on surprising and provocative display, he realized she wasn't mannish at all.

She still wasn't the kind of woman he normally took to bed, and he would never call her pretty. Even so, that brief stab of lust reassured him, made him realize this could work. He would make it work. Ana was intrigued, interested; she hadn't said no. He'd expected her to say no immediately, a gut reaction. But she hadn't betrayed her own desire—he'd seen it before, at dinner, a flaring in her eyes—as well as, perhaps, her own sense of logic.

When he'd spoken to Enrico about the match, the old man had been surprised but accepting.

'Ana is a practical girl,' he'd said after a moment. 'She will see the advantages.'

Vittorio could see her now, considering those advantages, wondering if the comforts he could give her outweighed the lack of feeling. And yet there would be feeling…affection, respect. He wanted to *like* Ana; he simply didn't want to love her.

And, Vittorio acknowledged with a surprised wryness, he would desire her. Somewhat, at least.

Ana took her shot and then stepped aside so Vittorio could take his. As he passed by her, he inhaled her scent; she wore no perfume and smelled of soap and something else, something impossible to define. Dirt, he realized after a moment and nearly missed his shot. She smelled of sunshine and soil, of the vineyard he'd seen her stride through only days ago, as if she owned the world, or at least all of it that mattered.

It was not a smell he normally associated with a woman.

He straightened, stepping back so Ana could take her shot, making sure to step close enough to her so his elbow brushed her breast, as if by accident, just to see how she reacted. And how *he* reacted. Ana drew her breath in sharply; Vittorio shifted his weight to ease the intensifying ache of need in his groin.

She was untouched, he was sure of it. Untouched and untamed. And, despite the terrible clothes, the complete lack of feminine guile or charm or artifice, at that moment he wanted her. He wanted her, and he wanted to marry her.

He *would*.

She won. Ana knew she should feel triumph at this victory, yet in the light of everything else she found she felt little at all.

'It seems I must concede the game,' Vittorio said as he replaced his cue stick in the holder. 'Congratulations. You did warn me.'

'So I did.' Ana replaced her cue stick as well. She felt awkward now the game of *stecca* was over; a glance at her watch told her it was nearly midnight. They hadn't spoken of the whole wretched business proposition in over an hour, and she wasn't sure she wanted to bring it up now.

'So,' Vittorio said briskly, 'you'll need a few days to think about my business proposition?'

Vittorio obviously did not share her reluctance. 'A few days?' Ana repeated, her voice rising to something close to a squawk. 'Vittorio, I don't think—'

'Surely you won't dismiss it out of hand?' he countered, cutting off the objection she hadn't even known how to finish. He leaned against the billiards table, smiling, at ease, his powerful forearms folded. 'That is not good business, Ana.'

'Perhaps I don't want my marriage to be business,' she replied a bit stiffly.

Vittorio's gaze dropped to her mouth. She could *feel* his eyes there, on her lips, almost as if he were touching her. She could imagine his finger tracing the outline of her lips even though he hadn't moved. *She* had; she'd parted her lips in a silent yearning invitation. Her body betrayed her again and again. 'I think it could be good between us, Ana,' he said softly. 'Good in so many ways.'

His words thrilled her. They shouldn't—words counted for so little—but they did. They gave her hope, made her wonder if Vittorio could see her as a woman. A woman he wanted not just with his mind, but with his body. Unlike Roberto.

'In fact,' he continued, his voice as soft and sinuous as silk, 'as we have just finished a game where you soundly trounced me, we could shake hands.'

Automatically, Ana stuck out her hand, ignoring the tiny flip-flop of disappointment at his sensible suggestion. This was how she did business, had been doing it for years. In a man's world, she acted like a man. It made sense. It made sense *now*.

'I said we *could*,' Vittorio said, his voice so soft, almost languorous, and yet with a little hint of amusement. 'I didn't say we would.' His eyes glittered, his own mouth parting as hers had, and he leaned forward so when she breathed in she inhaled his musky scent. 'Instead, how about a kiss?'

'A kiss?' Ana repeated blankly as if she didn't understand the word. But oh, she did—already she could imagine it, wanted it, *needed* it: the feel of Vittorio's lips on hers, hard and soft at the same time, his hands on her waist or even— 'That's not how I do business, Vittorio.'

'But this business is a little different, is it not? And we should perhaps make sure we suit. That we are,' he clarified in that soft, dangerous voice, 'in fact attracted to one another.'

Again, his words rippled through her with a frisson of excitement and hope; it was a heady, potent mix. Was he actually saying he could be attracted to her? That he *was*? 'I don't think that's a good idea,'

Ana said stubbornly, yet she heard the longing in her own voice. So did Vittorio.

He smiled. Although he hadn't moved—he was still leaning against the billiards table, his arms folded—he exuded a lethal grace and Ana could all too easily imagine him closing the distance between them, taking her into his arms and... For heaven's sake, she'd read too many romance novels. Had too many desperate dreams.

That was just what she *wanted* him to do.

'I think it's a very good idea.'

'You don't want to kiss me,' she said, meaning it as a blunt statement of fact. Yet, even as she said the words she was conscious of how Vittorio looked *now*. There was no lip-curl of disdain, no dismissive flick of the eyes. His eyes were dark, dilated, his cheeks suffused with colour. She felt the answering colour rise up in her own cheeks, flood through her own body.

'Oh, but I do,' he murmured, and Ana realized just how much she wanted him to want to kiss her. And she wanted it too; she'd realized that a long time ago, but now she knew she was going to do it. It had become both a challenge and a craving.

'All right, then,' she said and, smiling a little, her heart thudding sickly, she stepped forward, straight into his arms. She'd been moving too fast and Vittorio's hands came up to steady her, gripping her bare shoulders so she didn't smack straight into his chest. Still, she felt the hard length of his body against hers, every nerve and sinew leaping to life in a way they never had before. This was so new, so intimate, so *wonderful*.

His lips were a millimetre from hers as he whispered, 'I like that when you decide to do something, you do it completely, with your whole heart.'

'Yes, I do,' Ana answered, and kissed him. She wasn't a good kisser. She knew that; she'd had too little experience. She was unschooled, clumsy, her lips hard against his, pressing, not knowing what to do. Feeling a fool.

Then Vittorio opened his mouth, somehow softening his lips—how did he do that? Ana wondered fuzzily—before she stopped thinking at all. His tongue slipped into the warmth of her own mouth, surprising her and causing a deep lightning shaft of pleasure to go right through her belly and down to her toes. Her hands came up of their own accord and bunched on his shirt, pulling him closer so their hips collided and she felt the full evidence of his desire; he hadn't been lying. He *had* wanted to kiss her.

That knowledge thrilled her, consumed her with its wonderful truth. This was not a man who had been left cold by her kiss, by her body. His body had betrayed *him*. Right now, at least, he wanted her. As a woman.

A sense of power and triumph surged through her, making her bold. Her hands slid down the slippery fabric of his shirt to the curve of his backside, pulling him towards her. She heard Vittorio's little inhalation of shock and smiled against his lips. He moaned into her mouth.

His mouth remained on hers, exploring the contours of her tongue and teeth, nipping and sliding, the intimate invasion making Ana's head spin and her breath shorten. She'd never known kissing could be like this. The few chaste pecks and stolen smacks at the end of a date didn't compare, didn't even count—

And then it was over. Vittorio released her and Ana took a stumbling step backwards, her fingers flying to her swollen lips.

'Well…' she managed. Her mind was still fuzzy, her senses still consumed by what had just occurred. Then she looked at Vittorio and saw how smug he seemed. He was smiling as if he'd just proved something, and Ana supposed he had.

'I think that quite settles the matter, wouldn't you say?'

'Nothing's settled,' Ana retorted sharply. She wouldn't have her future decided by a simple kiss— even if there hadn't been anything simple about it at all. It had been amazing and affirming and even transforming, the evidence of Vittorio's desire changing everything—or at least it *could* change everything. 'You said I should have a few days to consider.'

'At least you want to consider it now,' Vittorio replied, and Ana knew nothing she said could take away his smug sense of superiority that he'd been able to kiss her senseless. He looked completely recovered, if he had been shaken by that kiss, which Ana suspected he had not. Not like she had. All right, he'd desired her—for a moment—but perhaps any man would react the same way when a woman threw herself at him, which was essentially what Ana had done.

Except Roberto hadn't. When she'd thrown herself at *him*, desperate to prove herself desirable, he'd remained as still and cold as a statue, as unmoved and emotionless as a block of cold marble. And when she'd finished—pressing herself against him, kissing those slack lips, he'd actually stepped back and said in a voice filled with affront, 'Ana, I never thought of you that way.' A pause, horrible, endless, and then the most damning words of all: 'How could I?'

Still, Ana thought, gazing at Vittorio with barely disguised hunger, was that brief stab of desire—that amazing kiss—enough to base a marriage on? Along with the respect and affection and everything else Vittorio had promised?

'I'll consider it,' she said at last. 'I didn't say I would say yes.'

'Of course.'

Ana touched her lips again, then dropped her hand, knowing how revealing that little gesture was. 'I should go home.'

'I'll have my driver take you.' Vittorio smiled wryly. 'I'm afraid I've drunk a bit too much whisky to handle a car myself, and of course I would never jeopardise your safety.'

Ana nodded in acceptance, and Vittorio pressed the button by the door again. Within seconds a servant appeared. He issued some quick instructions, and then turned back to Ana. 'I'll see you to the door.'

They didn't speak as he led her through several stone corridors back to the huge entryway of the castle. The doors were already open and a driver—in uniform, even at this hour—waited on the front step.

'So this is goodbye,' Ana said a bit unevenly.

Vittorio tucked a tendril of hair behind her ear, his fingers trailing her cheek. That smugness had left his eyes and he looked softer now, if only for a moment. 'For now.'

Ana tried not to react to the touch of his hand. She felt incredibly unsettled, uncertain, unable to believe that the kiss they had just shared was real, that it could possibly mean something. At least to her. She had a horrible sick feeling that Vittorio, inflamed by a bit of whisky, had been acting on his baser instincts, trying to prove that this marriage bargain could actually work.

And he'd almost convinced her that it could.

Too tired to think any more, Ana slipped into the interior of the limo—the Porsche, it seemed, was reserved for Vittorio's exclusive use—and laid her

KATE HEWITT 83

head back against the seat as the driver sped away
from Castle Cazlevara back to her home.

Vittorio watched the car disappear down the curving
drive with a deep, primal sense of satisfaction. He'd
as good as branded her with that kiss; she was his.
In a matter of days, weeks at the most, she would be
his bride. His wife. He felt sure of it.

He couldn't keep the sense of victory from rush-
ing through him, headier than any wine. He'd set out
to acquire a wife and, in a matter of days—a week
at the most—he would have one. Mission accomplished.

He imagined the look on his mother's face when
he told her he was getting married; he leaped ahead
to the moment when he held his son, and saw
Bernardo's dreams of becoming Count, of taking
control of Cazlevara Wines, crumble to nothing. He
pictured his mother looking stunned, lost, and then
the image suddenly changed of its own accord and
instead he saw her smiling into the face of his child,
her grandchild. A baby girl.

Vittorio banished the image almost instantly. It
didn't make sense. The only relationship he'd ever
had with his mother had been one of, at worst, ani-
mosity and, at best, indifference. And he didn't want
a girl; he needed sons.

Yet still the image—the idea—needled him, annoyed him, because it made a strange longing rise

up in a way he didn't understand, a way that almost felt like sorrow.

Vittorio pushed it aside once more and considered the practicalities instead. Of course, there were risks. With any business proposition, there were risks. Ana might not fall pregnant easily, or they might only have girls. Baby girls, all wrapped in pink—Vittorio dismissed these possibilities, too exultant to dwell on such concerns.

He supposed he should have married long ago and thus secured his position, yet he'd never even considered it. He'd been too intent on avoiding his home, on securing his own future. He'd never thought of his heirs.

He'd run away, Vittorio knew, the actions of a hurt child. Amazing how much power and pain those memories still held. His mother's averted face, the way she'd pushed him down when he'd attempted to clamber on her lap. He'd stopped trying after a while. By the time he was four—when Bernardo had been born—he'd regarded his mother with a certain wariness, the way you would a sleeping tiger in a zoo. Fascinating, beautiful, but ultimately dangerous. And now he was a grown man, nearing forty and he still remembered. He still hurt.

Self-contempt poured through him, dousing his earlier sense of victory. He hated this feeling, as if he was captive to his own past, chained by memories. Surely no man should still lament his childhood? Besides, his hadn't even been very deprived:

his father had loved him, had given him every opportunity and privilege. To feel sorry for himself in even the smallest degree was not only absurd, it was abhorrent.

Vittorio straightened his shoulders and pushed the memories back down.

Now he would run away no more. He'd come back to Veneto to finally face his family, his past and make it right in the only way he knew how. By moving on. His first family had failed him, so he would create a second. His own. His wife, his child. *His.*

His face hardening with determination, Vittorio turned back to the dark, empty castle and went inside.

CHAPTER FOUR

VILLA ROSSO was dark as the driver let her out at the front door. Ana tiptoed through the silent downstairs, wanting to avoid her father, even though she was fairly certain he was asleep. Enrico Viale didn't stay up much past ten.

She fell into bed, and then thankfully was fast sleep within minutes. When she awoke, the sun was slanting through the curtains, sending its long golden rays along the floor of her bedroom. Last night filtered back to her through a haze of sleep: the so-called business proposition, the billiards, the whisky, the *kiss*. She had no head for hard liquor at all. If she hadn't had that whisky, she wouldn't have kissed him, wouldn't have let him kiss her. Wouldn't now be wondering about all the possibilities—all the hopes—that kiss had given her, her body awakened to its natural longings, her soul singing with sudden, fierce joy—

Quickly, Ana swung out of bed and dressed. She strode downstairs, determined to put the thoughts and, more importantly, the treacherous desires

Vittorio Cazlevara created within her out of her mind completely, at least for a morning. They were too seductive, too dangerous, too *much*.

She stopped short when she saw her father in the dining room, eating toast and kippers. Her English mother, Emily, had insisted on a full English breakfast every day and, sixteen years after her death, Enrico still continued the tradition.

'Good morning!' he called brightly. 'You were out late last night. I waited up until eleven.'

'You shouldn't have.' Almost reluctantly, Ana came into the dining room, dropping her usual kiss on her father's head. She wasn't ready to talk to her father, to ask him how much he knew. She remembered his lack of surprise at Vittorio's return, or the fact that he'd asked her out to dinner. Had he known—could he possibly have imagined—just what the business proposition was? The thought sent something strange and alarming coursing through Ana's blood. She didn't know whether it was fear or joy, or something in between. Had Vittorio asked her father for his *blessing*? How long had he been planning this?

'Come, have some breakfast. The kippers are especially good this morning.'

Ana made a face as she grabbed a roll from the sideboard and poured herself a coffee from the porcelain pot left on the table. 'You know I can't abide kippers.'

'But they're so delicious,' Enrico said with a smile, and ate one.

Ana sat down opposite him, sipping her coffee even though it was too hot. 'I can only stay a moment,' she warned. 'I need to go down to the offices.'

'But Ana! It's Saturday.'

Ana shrugged; she often worked on Saturdays, especially in the busy growing season. 'The grapes don't stop for anyone, Papà.'

'How was your dinner with Vittorio?'

'Interesting.'

'He wanted to discuss business?' Enrico asked in far too neutral a tone.

Ana looked at him directly, daring him to be dishonest. 'Papà, did Vittorio speak to you about this—this business proposition of his?'

Enrico looked down, shredding a kipper onto his plate with the tines of his fork. 'Perhaps,' he said very quietly.

Ana didn't know whether to be disappointed or relieved or, even, strangely flattered. She felt a confusing welter of emotions, so she could only shake her head and ask with genuine curiosity, 'And what did you think of it?'

'I was surprised, at first.' He looked up, smiling wryly, although his eyes were serious. 'As I imagine you were.'

'Completely.' The single word was heartfelt.

'But then I thought about it—and Vittorio showed me the advantages—'

'What advantages?' What could Vittorio have said to convince her father that he should allow his daughter to marry him as a matter of convenience? For surely, Ana knew now, her father was convinced.

'Many, Ana. Stability, security.'

'I have those—'

'Children. Companionship.' He paused and then said softly, 'Happiness.'

'You think Vittorio Cazlevara could make me happy?' Ana asked. She didn't sound sceptical; she felt genuinely curious. She wanted to know. Could he make her happy? Why was she thinking this way? She'd been happy… Yet at that moment Ana couldn't pretend she didn't want more, that she didn't want the things her father had mentioned. Children. A home of her own. To kiss Vittorio again, to taste him…

Some last bastion of common sense must have remained for she burst out suddenly, 'We're talking about *marriage*, Papà.' Her voice broke on the word. 'A life commitment. Not some…some sort of transaction.' Even if Vittorio had presented it as such.

'What is your objection?' Enrico asked, his fingertips pressed together, his head cocked to one side. He'd always been a logical man; some would call him unemotional. Even after the death of his beloved wife, his calm exterior had barely cracked.

Ana remembered the one time he'd truly shown his grief, rocking and keening on Emily's bedroom floor; as a girl, the sudden, uncontrollable display of emotion had shocked her. He'd closed her off from it, slammed the door and then, with a far worse finality, shut himself off from her rather than let his daughter see him in such a state of emotional weakness. The separation at such a crucial time had devastated her.

It had been two years before they'd regained the relationship they'd once had.

Now she knew she couldn't really be surprised that he was approaching the issue of her possible marriage with such a cool head.

Vittorio's arguments would have appealed marvellously to his own sense of checks and balances. Indeed, she shared his sense of logic, prided herself on her lack of feminine fancy. After living with her father as her lone companion for most of her life, the sentimental theatrics of most women were cloying and abhorrent. She didn't, Ana reflected with a wry sorrow, even know how to be a woman.

Yet Vittorio had treated her as one, when he'd kissed her...

Even so. *Marriage*...

'My objection,' she said, 'is the entire idea of marriage as a business proposition. It seems so cold.'

'But surely it doesn't have to be? Better to go into such an enterprise with a clear head, reasonable expectations—'

'I still don't even understand why Vittorio wants to marry me—' Ana said, stopping suddenly, wishing she hadn't betrayed herself. Just like her father, she hated to be vulnerable. She knew what it felt like to be so exposed, so raw, and then so rejected.

'He needs a wife. He must be in his late thirties, you know, and a man starts to think of his future, his children—'

'But why me?' The words came, as unstoppable as the fears and doubts that motivated them. 'He could have anyone, anyone at all—'

'Why not you, Ana?' Enrico asked gently. 'You would make any man a wonderful wife.'

Ana's mouth twisted. Her father also called her *dolcezza*. Sweet little thing. He was her father, her *papà*; of course he believed such things. That didn't mean *she* believed them, or him. 'Still, there would be no love involved.'

Enrico gave a little shrug. 'In time, it comes.'

She was shredding her roll onto her plate, just as her father had done with his poor little kipper. Her appetite—what little there had been of it—had completely vanished. She looked up at her father and shook her head. 'With Vittorio, I don't think so.' Her throat went tight, and she cursed herself for a fool. She didn't *need* love. She'd convinced herself of that long ago. She didn't even want it, and she couldn't fathom why she'd mentioned it to her father.

Her father remained unfazed. 'Still, affection. Respect. These things count for much, *dolcezza*. More perhaps than you can even imagine now, when love seems so important.'

'Yet you loved Mamma.'

Her father nodded, his face seeming to crumple just a little bit. Even sixteen years on, he still lived for her memory.

'Don't you think I want that kind of love too?' Ana asked, her voice turning raw. Despite what she'd said—what she believed—she needed to know her father's answer.

Enrico didn't speak for a moment. He poured himself another cup of coffee and sipped it thoughtfully. 'That kind of love,' he finally said, 'is not easy. It is not comfortable.'

'I never said I wanted to be comfortable.'

'Comfort,' Enrico told her with a little smile, 'is always underrated by those who have experienced nothing else.'

'Are you saying you weren't…comfortable…with Mamma?' The idea was a novel one, and one Ana didn't like to consider too closely. She'd always believed her parents to have had the grandest of love matches, adoring each other to the end. A fairy tale, and one she'd clung to in those first dark days of grief. Yet now her father seemed to be implying something else.

'I loved her,' Enrico replied. 'And I was happy. But comfortable, always? No. Your mother was a wonderful woman, Ana, be assured of that. But she was emotional—and I'm the one who is Italian!' He smiled, the curve of his mouth tinged with a little sadness. 'It was not always easy to live with someone who felt things so deeply.' Snatches of memory came to her, swirls of colour and sound. Her mother crying, the cloying scent of a sick room, the murmurs of a doctor as her father shook his head. And then her mother pulling her close, whispering fervently against her hair how she, Ana, would be the only one, the only child. Love, Ana thought, did not protect you from sorrow. Perhaps it only softened the blow.

Enrico put down his coffee cup and gave Ana a level look. 'Be careful to realize what you would be giving up by not marrying Vittorio, Ana.'

Ana drew back, stung. 'What are you saying? That I might as well take the best offer—the only offer—I can get?'

'No, of course I am not saying that,' Enrico said gently. 'But it is a very good offer.'

Ana sipped her coffee, moodily acknowledging the truth of her father's words. She'd only given voice to her own fears—that there would be no other offers. Would she rather live alone, childless, lonely—because, face it, she *was*—than attempt some kind of marriage with Vittorio? She didn't know the answer. She could hardly believe she was actually asking herself the question.

'Vittorio is a good man,' Enrico said quietly.

'How do you know?' Ana challenged. 'He's been away for fifteen years.'

'I knew his father. Vittorio was the apple of

Arturo's eye. Arturo was a good man too, but he was hard.' Enrico frowned a little. 'Without mercy.'

'And what if Vittorio is the same?' She remembered the steely glint in his eye and wondered just how well she knew him. Not well at all, was the obvious answer. Certainly not well enough to marry him.

And yet…he *was* a good man. She felt that in her bones, in a certain settling of her soul. She believed her father and, more importantly, she believed Vittorio.

It's all right to be sad, rondinella.

'Vittorio needs a wife to soften him,' Enrico said with a smile.

'I don't want him to be my project,' Ana protested. 'Or for me to be his.' She was so prickly, had been so ever since Vittorio had proposed—if you could call it proposing. The word conjured images of roses and diamond rings and declarations of undying love. Not a cold-blooded contract.

'Of course not,' Enrico agreed, 'but you know, in marriage, you are each other's projects. You don't seek to change each other, but it is hoped that you will affect one another, shape and smooth each other's rough edges.'

Ana made a face. 'You make it sound like two rocks in a stream.'

'But that's exactly it,' Enrico exclaimed. 'Two rocks rubbing along together in the river of life.'

Ana let out a reluctant laugh. 'Now, really, Papà,

you are waxing far too philosophical for me. I must get to work.' She rose from the table, kissing him again, and went to get her shoes and coat; a light spring drizzle was falling.

Once at the winery, she immersed herself in what she loved best. Business. *Just like Vittorio*, a sly little voice inside her mind whispered, but Ana pushed it away. She wasn't going to think about Vittorio or marriage or any of it until noon, at least.

In fact, she barely lifted her head from the papers scattered over her desk until Edoardo knocked on her door in the late afternoon. 'A package, Signorina Viale.'

'A package?' Ana blinked him into focus. 'You mean a delivery?'

'Not for the winery,' Edoardo said. 'It is marked personal. For you. It was dropped off—by the Count of Cazlevara.'

Ana stilled, her heart suddenly pounding far too fiercely. Vittorio had been here, had sent her something? Anticipation raced through her, made her dizzy with longing. Somehow she managed to nod stiffly, with apparent unconcern, and raised one hand to beckon him. 'Bring it in, please.'

The box was white, long and narrow and tied with a satin ribbon in pale lavender. Roses, Ana thought. It must be. She felt mingled disappointment and anticipation; roses were beautiful, but when it came to flowers they were expected and a bit, well, ordinary. It didn't take much thought to send a woman roses.

Still, she hadn't received roses or any other flowers in years, so she opened the box with some excitement, only to discover he hadn't sent roses at all.

He'd sent grapes.

She stared at the freshly cut vines with their cluster of new, perfect, pearl-like grapes and then bent her head to breathe in their wonderful earthy scent. There was a stiff little card nestled among the leaves. Ana picked it up and read:

A new hybrid of Vinifera and Rotundifolia, from the Americas, that I thought you'd be interested in.—V.

She flicked the card against her fingers and then, betrayingly, pressed it against her lips. It smelled fresh and faintly pungent, like the grapes. She closed her eyes. This, she realized, was much better than roses, and she had a feeling Vittorio knew it.

Was this his way of romancing her? Or simply convincing her? Showing her the benefits of such business?

Did it even matter? He'd done it; he'd known what she'd like, and Ana found she was pleased.

For the rest of the day Ana immersed herself in work, determined not to think of Vittorio or the spray of grapes that remained on her desk, in plain view. Yet she couldn't quite keep the thoughts—the hopes—from slipping slyly into her mind. She found herself constructing a thousand what-ifs. *What if we married? What if we had a child? What if we actually were happy?*

These thoughts—tempting, dangerous—continued to dance along the fringes of her mind over the next week. She caught herself more than once, chin in hand, lost in a daydream that was vague enough to seem reasonable. Possible. She found she was arguing with herself, listing the reasons why a marriage of convenience was perfectly sensible. Why it was, in fact, a good idea.

She didn't see Vittorio all week, but every day there was something from him: a newspaper article on a new wine, a bar of dark chocolate—how did he know that was her secret indulgence?—a spray of lilacs. Ana accepted each gift, found herself savouring them, even as she knew why he was doing it. It was, undoubtedly, a means to an end, a way of showing her how it could be between them.

I think it could be good between us, Ana... Good in so many ways.

Remembering how it had felt to kiss him—how he'd felt, the evidence of his own arousal—made Ana agree with him. Or, at least, want to agree with him. And want to experience it again.

A week after her dinner with Vittorio, as the day came to a close, the sun starting its orange descent, Ana left the winery office and decided to walk the half-kilometre home along the winding dirt track, her mind still brimming with those seductive what-ifs. A new wealth of possibilities was opening up to her, things she'd never hoped to have. A husband, a child, a home, a life beyond what she'd already made for herself, what she'd been happy to have until Vittorio stirred up these latent desires like a nest of writhing serpents. Ana wondered if they could ever be coaxed to sleep again.

If she said no, could she go back to her life with the endless work days and few evenings out among old men and fellow winemakers? Could she lull to sleep those deep and dangerous desires for a husband, a family, a home—a castle, even—of her own? Could she stop craving another kiss and, more than that, so much more, the feel of another's body against hers, that wonderful spiral of desire uncoiling and rising within her, demanding to be sated?

No, Ana acknowledged, she couldn't, not easily anyway and, even more revealingly, she didn't want to. She wanted to feel Vittorio's lips against hers again. She wanted to know the touch of his hands on her body. She wanted to be married, to live and learn together like the two stones her father had been talking about.

Even if there was no love. She didn't need it.

Stopping suddenly right there in the road, Ana laughed aloud. Was her decision already made? Was she actually going to marry Vittorio?

No. Surely she couldn't make such a monumental decision so quickly, so carelessly. Surely her life was worth more than that.

Yet, even as common sense argued its case, her

heart and body were warring against it, lost in a world of wonderful—and sensual—possibility.

Slowly, she started walking again; the sun was low in the sky, sending long lavender rays across the horizon. Villa Rosso appeared in the distance, its windows winking in the sunlight, its long, low stone façade so familiar and dear. If she married Vittorio, she wouldn't live there any more. Her father would be alone. The thought stopped her once more in the road; could she do that? Could she leave her father after all they'd shared and endured together? She knew he would want her to do so; this marriage—should it happen—already had his blessing.

Still, it would be hard, painful even. It made her realize afresh just how enormous a decision she was contemplating.

Could she actually say yes? Was she brave—and foolish—enough to do it?

As she came closer to the house, she saw a familiar navy Porsche parked in the drive. Vittorio's car. He was inside, waiting for her, and the realization made her insides flip right over. She'd *missed* him, she realized incredulously; she'd expected him to come before now.

She'd *wanted* him to come.

At the front step she took a moment to brush the hair away from her face and wipe the dust from her shoes before she opened the door and stepped into the foyer.

It was empty, but she followed the voices into the

study, where she checked at the sight of Vittorio and her father in what looked like a cosy tête-à-tête. Enrico looked up and smiled as she entered, and Vittorio stood.

'We were just talking about you,' Enrico said with a little smile and, despite the treacherous beating of her heart, Ana smiled rather coolly back.

'Were you? What a surprise.'

'I came to see if you'd like to have dinner with me,' Vittorio said. He seemed entirely unruffled at being caught gossiping about her with her father.

Ana hesitated. She wanted to have dinner with Vittorio again but suddenly she also felt uncertain, afraid. Of what, she could not even say. She was afraid to rush, to show her own eagerness. She needed time to sort her thoughts and perhaps even to steel her heart. 'I'm not dressed—'

'No matter.'

She glanced down at her grey wool trousers and plain white blouse—which, aggravatingly, had become untucked. Again. 'Really?'

Vittorio arched his eyebrows, a smile playing around his mouth. 'Really.' And, though he said nothing more, Ana knew he was surmising that she had a wardrobe of similarly unappealing clothes upstairs. At least they were clean and freshly ironed.

Still, she accepted the challenge. Why should she change for Vittorio? Why should she attempt to look pretty—if such a thing could be done—for the sake of this business arrangement? She lifted her chin.

'Fine. Let me just wash my face and hands at least.'
He nodded, and Ana walked quickly from the room,
trying to ignore the hurt that needled her, the little
sink of her heart at his indifference to her clothes,
her appearance. She wanted Vittorio to care how she
looked. She wanted him to *like* how she looked.

Get over it, her mind told her, the words hard and
determined. *If you're going to marry him, this is how
it is going to be.*

Her heart sank a little further. She wished it
hadn't.

Within just a few minutes they were speeding
down the darkening drive, away from Villa Rosso,
the windows open to the fragrant evening air.

'Where are we going?' Ana asked as the hair she'd
just tidied blew into tangles around her face.

'Venice.'

'Venice!' she nearly yelped. 'I'm not dressed for
that—'

Vittorio's glance was hooded yet smiling. 'Let me
worry about that.'

Ana sat back, wondering just how and why Vittorio
was going to worry about her clothes. The idea made
her uneasy.

She found out soon enough. Vittorio parked the
Porsche at Fusina and they boarded a ferry for the
ten-minute ride into the city that allowed no cars.
As the worn stone buildings and narrow canals with
their sleepy-looking gondolas and ancient arched
bridges came into view, Ana felt a frisson of expec-

tation and even hope. What city was more romantic than Venice? And just why was Vittorio taking her here?

After they disembarked, he led her away from the Piazza San Marco, crowded with tourists, to Frezzeria, a narrow street lined with upscale boutiques. Most of them had already closed, but all it took was Vittorio rapping once on the glass door of one for the clerk inside, a chic-looking woman with hair in a tight chignon, wearing a silk blouse and a black pencil skirt, to open the door and kiss him on both cheeks.

A ridiculous, totally unreasonable dart of jealousy stabbed Ana, and fury followed it when the woman swept her assessingly critical gaze over her and said, 'This is the one?'

'Yes.'

She snapped her fingers. 'Come with me.'

Ana turned to Vittorio, her eyes narrowed. 'You talked about me?' she said in an angry undertone, choosing to show anger over the hurt she felt inside, a raw, open wound to the heart. She could only imagine the conversation Vittorio must have had with this woman, talking about her hopeless clothes, her terrible taste, how pathetic and *ugly* she was...

She tasted bile, swallowed. What a fool she'd been.

'She's here to help you, Ana,' Vittorio murmured. 'Go with her.'

Ana could see racks of gorgeous-looking clothes—

a rainbow of silks and satins—in the back of the boutique. They beckoned to her, surprisingly, because she'd never been a girly kind of woman. She'd avoided all things feminine, mostly out of necessity. She didn't want to look ridiculous. Yet the enticement of the clothes was no match for the hurt—and fury—she felt now.

'Perhaps I don't want help,' she snapped. 'Did you ever consider that?'

Vittorio remained unfazed. 'Is that true?' he asked calmly, so clearly confident of the answer. Humiliatingly, his gaze raked over her, more eloquent than anything he could have said. Ana's cheeks burned.

The woman appeared once more in the doorway, her lips pursed in impatience. She was holding a gown over one arm, frothy with lace. Ana had never seen anything so beautiful. She could not imagine wearing such a thing, or what she would look like in it. It could not possibly be her size.

'Ana,' Vittorio murmured, 'you will look beautiful in these clothes. Surely you want to look beautiful?'

'Perhaps I just want to be myself,' Ana said quietly. She didn't add that she was afraid she *wouldn't* look beautiful in those clothes, or that she wished he thought she looked beautiful already. It was too difficult to explain, too absurd even to feel. She didn't want Vittorio to want to change her, even if she was willing to be changed. Stupid, unreasonable, perhaps, but true. She shook her head and pushed past him to the door. 'I'm sorry, Vittorio, but I'm not going to be your Cinderella project.'

Vittorio stifled a curse as he called back to Feliciana before following Ana out into the street. He'd thought she would appreciate the clothes, the opportunity to look, for once, like a woman. He'd thought he was giving her a *gift*. Instead, she acted offended. Would he ever understand women? Vittorio wondered in annoyed exasperation. He'd *thought* he understood women; he was certainly good with them. Allow them unlimited access to clothes and jewels and they'd love you for ever—or think they did.

Not that he wanted Ana's love, but her gratitude would have been appreciated at this point. He gazed at her, her arms wrapped around herself, her hair blowing in the breeze off the canal, and wondered if he'd ever understand her. He'd thought it would be simple, easy. He'd thought her an open book, to be read—and discarded—at his own leisure. The realization that she was far more complicated, that he'd managed to dismiss her before even getting to know her, was both annoying and shaming.

'I think perhaps you should take me home.'

'We have reservations at one of the finest restaurants in Venice,' Vittorio said, his voice clipped, his teeth gritted. 'That's why I brought you to this boutique—so you could be dressed appropriately, preferably in a dress!'

'If you want to marry me,' Ana replied evenly, 'then you need to accept me as I am. I won't change for you, Vittorio.'

'Not even your clothes?' He couldn't keep the caustic note out of his voice. The woman was impossible. And, damnation, she was blinking back tears. He hadn't meant to make her cry; the last thing he needed now was *tears*. He'd hurt her, and his annoyance and shame deepened, cutting him. Hurting *him*. 'Ana—'

She shook her head, half-talking to herself. 'I don't know why I ever thought—hoped, even—that this could work. You don't know me at all. We're *strangers*—'

'Of course I don't know you!' he snapped. Impatience bit at him, the swamping sense of his own failure overtook him. He'd lost control of the situation, and he had no idea how it had happened. When she'd come into the villa this evening and he'd seen how her eyes had lit at the sight of him, he'd felt so confident. So sure that she was going to marry him, that she'd already said yes in her mind, if not her heart. Hearts need not be involved.

Yet, even as Vittorio reminded himself of this, he realized how impossible a situation this truly was. He wanted to be kind to Ana; he wanted affection and respect to bud and grow. He wanted her loyalty; he just didn't want her to fall in love with him.

Yet there seemed no danger of that right now.

'I thought,' he finally said, 'this could be an opportunity for us to get to know one another.'

'After you've changed me.'

'After I bought you a dress!' Vittorio exploded. 'Most women would have been thrilled—'

'Well, I'm not most women,' Ana snapped. Her cheeks glowed with colour and her eyes were a steely grey. She looked, Vittorio thought with a flash of surprise, magnificent. Like a woman warrior, Boadicea, magnificent in her self-righteous anger, and all that vengeful fury was directed at him. 'And *most* women I know,' she spat, 'wouldn't entertain your business proposition for a single minute!' With that, her eyes still shooting angry sparks at him, she turned on her heel and stormed down Frezzeria towards the Piazza.

This time Vittorio cursed aloud.

Standing alone, crowds of tourists pushing past her, Ana wondered if she should have gone back with that stick-thin saleswoman and tried on those gorgeous clothes. In one part of her mind—the part that still managed to remain cool and logical—she knew Vittorio had been trying to please her. Surprise her with a gift. It would have been the kind thing—the sensible thing—to accept it and go back into that dressing room. Part of her had even wanted to.

And part of her had been afraid to, and another part had wished Vittorio didn't want to improve her. No matter what her father had said about smoothing stones and that ridiculous river of life, she didn't want Vittorio to improve her. She wouldn't be his little project.

And if he was thinking of marrying her—if she was actually still considering marrying him—then she knew he needed to accept that. Accept *her*.

She'd only walked a few metres before Vittorio caught up, grabbing her by the arm none too gently. 'How are you planning on returning home?' he asked, his voice coldly furious and, angry again, Ana shrugged off his arm.

'Fortunately, there are such things as water taxis.'

'Ana—' Vittorio stopped helplessly and Ana knew he was utterly bewildered by her behaviour. Well, that made two of them. She stopped walking, her head bowed.

'I know you think you meant well,' she began, only to stop when Vittorio laughed dryly.

'Oh, dear,' he said. 'I've *really* botched it then, haven't I?'

She looked up, trying to smile. 'I just—' She took a breath, trying to explain without making herself utterly vulnerable. It was impossible. 'I don't wear dresses for a reason, Vittorio. It's not simply that I have appalling taste in clothes.' He looked so surprised, she almost laughed. 'Is that what you thought? That I don't know a designer gown from a bin bag?'

'I didn't—' he began, and now she did laugh. She'd

never expected to see the Count of Cazlevara so dis-comfited.

'I'm a full-figured five foot eleven,' she said flatly. 'Designer gowns generally don't run in my size.'

Surprise flashed briefly in Vittorio's eyes. 'I think,' he said quietly, 'you are selling yourself a bit short.'

'I prefer not to sell myself at all,' she returned rather tartly.

Someone tapped her on the shoulder and Ana turned. 'Would you mind moving? I'm trying to get a snap of San Marco,' a camera-toting tourist explained and, muttering an oath, Vittorio took Ana by the arm once more and led her away from the crowded piazza.

'We can't have a conversation here—let's go to dinner, as I originally suggested.'

'But I'm not dressed appropriately—'

Vittorio gave her an arch look. 'And whose fault is that?'

'Yours,' she replied but, instead of sounding ac-cusing, her voice came out pert, almost as if she were flirting. Except, Ana thought, she didn't know how to flirt. Yet Vittorio was smiling a little and so was she. 'If you'd let me change,' she continued in that same pert voice, 'instead of trying to turn a sow's ear into a—'

'Don't.' Suddenly, surprisingly, his hand came up to cover her mouth. Ana could taste the salt on his skin. 'Don't insult yourself, Ana.' His expression had softened, his mouth curved in something close to a smile, except it was too serious and even sad. She tried to speak, her lips moving against his fingers, but he wouldn't let her. 'I'm taking you to dinner,' he stated, 'no matter what you're wearing. Anyone who is with the Count of Cazlevara doesn't need to worry about clothes.' He smiled and his thumb caressed the fullness of her lower lip, the simple touch sending shockwaves of pleasure down into her belly. 'You'll find that's one of the advantages of becoming a Countess,' he said, and dropped his hand.

CHAPTER FIVE

ONCE seated at the best table at the Met, one of Venice's finest restaurants, Ana took in the glamorous couples all around them, the women all in designer gowns like the one she could have worn, and she felt another shaft of regret that she'd spurned Vittorio's generous offer of a dress. Even if it had been the safe—and even the right—thing to do.

Still, Vittorio seemed utterly unperturbed by the difference between her own attire and that of every other woman in the room. He gazed down at the menu, tapping it with one finger. 'The mussels are particularly good.'

'I'll keep that in mind.' Now that she was here, seated across from Vittorio, contemplating actually *marrying* him...Ana swallowed. Her throat felt bone-dry. She felt as if she were poised to jump off a cliff and she had no idea what waited underneath her, water or rocks, life or death.

They chose from the menu—Ana decided on chicken over fish—and Vittorio ordered the wine, a local vintage, of course, although not one of either of theirs. 'Always good to consider the competition,' he said with a smile, and Ana nodded. She did the same when she dined out, which admittedly wasn't all that often.

When their first courses arrived and the wine had been poured, Ana gave Vittorio as direct a look as she could and said, 'I have some questions.'

Vittorio took a sip of wine. 'Very well.'

Nerves made her hands slippery around her wine glass and her voice came out a little breathless. 'What would you expect of…of a wife?'

Vittorio's expression was annoyingly inscrutable. He took another sip of wine, cocking his head to regard Ana thoughtfully. 'I'd expect my wife to be a life partner,' he said finally. 'In every sense.'

The answer, so simple, so honest, made Ana feel even more breathless and her cheeks heated. She looked down. 'Without knowing me, that's quite a big gamble.' She looked up at him again, searching for some clue to his emotions, trying to discover just why he had, over all women, chosen her in this surely coveted role.

'It's not,' Vittorio said after a moment, 'as big a gamble as you think.'

'What do you mean?'

He shrugged. 'I'm not about to embark on one of my life's major decisions without any knowledge at all, Ana. I did some research.'

'Research?' she practically spluttered. 'On me?'

'Of course.' He smiled, amused by her outrage.

'And you can research me if you like. As I said, we are each other's best assets.' He sat back, still smiling, and Ana found she was annoyed at his smug confidence. He was so very sure that any research she did would show him to advantage and, annoyingly, she was quite sure of it too.

'What did you learn?' she finally asked, her voice stiff with dignity.

'That you are a hard worker. That you are healthy—'

'You accessed my medical records?' Ana squawked, wondering how he had managed to do *that*, and Vittorio gave a negligent shrug. Nothing, apparently, was beyond the power—or the pale—for the Count of Cazlevara.

'Now I really feel like a horse,' she muttered. 'Would you like to see my teeth as well?'

'I see them when you speak,' Vittorio replied with a little smile. 'They're very nice.'

Ana just shook her head. Was there any aspect of her life—her body—that he had not researched and inspected? Should she be honoured that she'd passed all these nameless tests? She wasn't. She was furious and, worse, she felt horribly vulnerable, as if Vittorio had spied on her when she was naked. At least he seemed to have liked what he'd seen.

'I also learned,' Vittorio continued blandly, 'that you are passionate about wine and this region. That you are a good friend to those who know you. And, most importantly, that you are loyal.'

She looked up in curiosity and surprise, remembering how he'd spoken of loyalty the other night. 'And loyalty is so important to you?'

'It is,' Vittorio said and his voice, though still low and modulated, seemed suddenly to vibrate with intensity, 'paramount.'

Ana stared, trying to digest this new bit of information. Loyalty was surely so important mainly to those who had once been betrayed. What had happened to Vittorio? 'Are you speaking of fidelity?' she asked.

'No, although of course I would expect you to be faithful to me and our marriage vows. I speak of another kind of loyalty. I would expect you to stand by me and the decisions I make, never to take another's position against me.' His dark eyes caught and held hers. 'Can you do that, Ana? It will not always be easy.'

The conversation that had started so matter-of-fact had suddenly become emotional, intense. Dark. 'If you mean will I never question you—'

His hand slashed through the air. 'I'm not asking for blind obedience. I want a wife, not a lapdog. But you must realize that, because of my position and my wealth, there are those who seek to discredit me. They would even enlist your aid, attract your sympathy by the foulest and most devious motives. Can you—will you—be loyal to me against those enemies?'

Ana suppressed a shiver. She wanted to make a

joke of it, tell Vittorio to stop being so melodramatic, yet she had the terrible feeling that he was deadly serious. 'Vittorio—'

'I mean all that I say, Ana,' he said quietly. He reached across the table to encircle her wrist with his hand, his fingers pressing against her bare skin. Nerves jumped at the touch. 'I can tell you think I exaggerate, that I am seeing shadows where there is only light. But I will tell you that the quality that attracted me to you most of all was your sense of loyalty. You've lived with your father for nearly ten years, ever since you returned from university. You've helped him and taken care of him in a way that is gentle and beautiful. Of course, he is your father and he commands your loyalty because of his role. I will ask you now—do you think you can give such allegiance to me?'

'If I were married to you,' Ana said slowly, 'then, yes.'

Vittorio released her wrist and sat back with a deeply satisfied smile. 'Then I know all I need to know. Now it is your turn to ask questions of me.'

'All right,' Ana said, still a bit shaken by the intensity of their exchange. 'If we were married, I would still expect to work for Viale Wines. Would that be acceptable to you?'

Vittorio lifted a shoulder in assent. 'Of course. Naturally, I would expect our children to take the reins of both the Cazlevara and Viale labels. Truly, an empire.'

Ana nodded slowly. *Children*. Under the table, she pressed a hand against her middle. 'And my father,' she said after a moment. 'Of course, he would still live at Villa Rosso, but I would want to see him often, and invite him to be with us whenever possible.'

'Naturally.'

A bubble of sudden nervous laughter escaped her and she shook her head. 'This is so crazy.'

'It seems so, I agree, but actually it makes wonderful sense.'

And she was a sensible person, which was why she was considering it all. Because it was so logical. It just didn't feel that way at the moment. It didn't feel logical when he kissed her.

It felt wonderful.

'I'm scared,' she whispered, her voice so low she didn't know if Vittorio had heard her. She didn't know if she wanted him to.

In fact, she thought he hadn't heard her, for he didn't reply; then she felt his hand on hers, his fingers warm on her skin, curling around her own fingers, squeezing slightly. She took a deep breath and let it out in a shuddering sigh. 'I never thought I'd marry, you know.'

'Why not?' Vittorio asked, his voice as quiet as hers.

Ana shrugged, not wanting to explain. Vittorio squeezed her fingers again, and she felt a lump at the back of her throat. 'What if we end up hating each other?'

'I have too much faith in both of us for that.'

'But we might—' she persisted, her mind coming up with every possibility, every consideration, now that she was actually at the moment of decision. Now that she was ready to jump.

'All good business decisions require a certain amount of risk, Ana. They also take courage and determination.' He smiled and released her hand to take a sip of wine. 'I recently closed a deal with several major hotels in Brazil. South America has never imported much Italian wine, and some would have said I was wasting time and money going there.' He leaned forward. 'But, when I went there, I did so knowing I would do anything to make it succeed. Once the decision is made, all it requires is a certain amount of persistence and follow-through.'

What clinical terms, Ana thought. Although she knew Vittorio meant them to be comforting, she found a certain coldness settling inside her instead. 'This really is…business.'

'Of course.' He glanced at her sharply. 'I told you last week, I'm not interested in love. You agreed with me. If you were not telling the truth—'

'I was.' Ana swallowed. 'Why?' she whispered. When Vittorio simply looked nonplussed, she continued, her voice only a bit ragged, 'Why do you not want to fall in love?'

He didn't answer for a long moment. 'Love,'

Vittorio finally said, his voice flat, 'is a destructive emotion.'

'It doesn't have to be—'

'Invariably, because we are all imperfect people, it becomes so. Trust me, Ana, I have seen it happen.' He swivelled his glass between his palms. 'Time and time again.'

'You've been in love, then?' Ana asked, her voice small, far too small and sad. Vittorio shook his head and she felt an absurd leap of relief.

'No. Because I have never wanted to be. But don't think that a loveless marriage must therefore be joyless. We will have affection, respect—'

'You sound like you've been speaking to my father.'

'He is a wise man.'

'He loved my mother,' Ana countered a bit defiantly.

'And yet he recommends you marry me?' There was only the faintest questioning lilt to Vittorio's voice and he smiled, leaning back once more, utterly confident. He arched an eyebrow. 'Why are you not interested in love, then?'

'I was in love once,' Ana said after a moment. She saw shock ripple across Vittorio's features before it was replaced by his usual bland composure. She wondered at her own answer. She didn't think she'd actually *loved* Roberto, but he had hurt her. 'I decided not to experience it again.'

'This man—he hurt you?'

'Yes. He…he decided he…' She faltered, not wanting to spell it out. *I never thought of you that way. How could I?* She'd left Roberto utterly cold, and Ana felt cold herself just remembering it. At least Vittorio desired her, to some degree. She could not deceive herself that he felt even an ounce of the overwhelming attraction she experienced with him, but at least he felt *something*. He wouldn't have kissed her otherwise. He wouldn't have responded to her own clumsy kiss.

That, at least, was something. Something small, pathetically so, perhaps, but it was more than Ana had ever had with a man before.

'We need not discuss it,' Vittorio said, covering her hand briefly with his own. Ana heard a hardness in his voice and his eyes flashed darkly. 'That man is in the past. We are forging something new, something good.'

'You sound so sure.'

'I am.' Ana just shook her head, still too overwhelmed by the speed with which these negotiations had been conducted. 'Why is it so difficult?' Vittorio asked. His voice remained bland, reasonable, yet Ana thought she heard the bite of impatience underneath. He'd made up his mind ages ago; he'd decided he wanted a wife and so he immediately went out and acquired one. For Vittorio, without the complications of any emotions, it was easy. Simple. 'There is no one else now,' he asked sharply, 'is there?'

She looked up, surprised. 'You know there isn't.'

'Then surely I am the best candidate.'

'If I even want a candidate,' she returned, her tone sharpening too. 'Perhaps living alone would be better.'

Vittorio's lips twisted wryly. 'Ouch.'

Ana's own mouth curved in a reluctant smile; even now he could make her laugh. 'What's your favourite colour?' she asked suddenly, and Vittorio raised his brows.

'Blue.'

'Do you like to read?'

'Paperback thrillers, my secret weakness.' He leaned back, seeming to enjoy this little exchange. Ana searched her mind for more questions; she should have dozens, hundreds, yet in the face of Vittorio's sexy little smile her mind was blanking horribly.

'Do you like dogs?'

'Yes, but not cats.'

'What food do you like?'

'Seafood. Chocolate. I keep a bar of dark chocolate in the kitchen freezer for my own personal use.' He was still smiling that incredible little smile that melted Ana's insides like that bar of dark chocolate left out in the sun.

'What food could your mother never get you to eat?'

His smile faltered for the merest of seconds, barely more than a flash, yet Ana saw it. Felt it. 'Broccoli.'

He loosened his collar with one finger. 'Now I'm almost embarrassed.'

'For not liking broccoli?' Ana returned, smiling too. 'Surely you have more secrets than that.'

Vittorio's lips twitched even as his eyes darkened. 'A few.'

She thought about asking other questions. *What makes your expression change like that, darkening as if the sun has disappeared? What memories are you hiding? How many lovers have you had? Why do you think love is destructive?* She swallowed, forcing them away, knowing that now was not the time. 'Tell me something about you that I'd never guess.'

'I play the trombone.'

She laughed aloud, the sound incredulous and merry. 'Really?'

Vittorio nodded solemnly. 'You had to take music lessons at school, and the trombone was the only instrument left in the music cupboard.'

'Were you any good?'

'Awful. I sounded like a dying sheep. My music teacher begged me to stop eventually, and I played football instead, thank God.'

Ana pressed her lips together against another laugh, and shook her head a little bit. *Don't make me fall in love with you.* She pushed the thought aside. 'If you could go anywhere or do anything, what would it be?'

His little smile widened into something almost feral, his eyes glinting in the candlelight. 'Marry you.'

Her heart leaped and she shook her head. 'Be serious.'

'I am.'

'Only because I tick the right boxes.'

'I have a lot of boxes.'

'Just when did you decide I was such a suitable candidate?' Ana asked. She looked up to see Vittorio tilt his head and narrow his eyes; it was a look she was becoming used to. It meant he was thinking carefully about what to say…and what he thought she wanted to hear.

'Does it matter?'

'I'm curious.'

He gave a tiny shrug. 'I've already told you, I first read about you in the in-flight magazine. It was a short article, but it piqued my interest.'

'Enough to dig into my background?' Ana guessed, and Vittorio's mouth tightened. He gestured to the waiter to take their plates, and the man scurried forward.

'I don't particularly like your tone or your choice of words,' he said calmly. 'I've been honest from the beginning.'

'That's true.' Yet, for some reason, his honesty hurt all the more. 'It's just so…cold-blooded.'

'Funny,' Vittorio said, taking a sip of wine, 'I thought you said you weren't a romantic.'

'I'm not,' Ana said quickly. She wondered whether she was lying. Had she actually been waiting for her knight in shining armour all this time? Was she really such a lovelorn fool?

No. She would not allow herself the weakness.

'Then what is the trouble?'

'It is a big decision, Vittorio,' Ana replied, a hint of sharpness to her tone. 'As you said before. I don't make such decisions lightly.' She took a breath. If he wanted businesslike, then that was what he would get. 'What about a pre-nuptial agreement?'

Vittorio arched his eyebrows. 'Are you worried I'll take your fortune?' he asked dryly, for the Viale wealth was a fraction of his.

'No, but I thought you might have that concern.'

Vittorio's mouth hardened into a thin line. 'Divorce is not an option.'

Ana swallowed. 'What if you meet someone else?'

'I won't.' The steely glint in those dark eyes kept Ana from even asking the question about whether she would.

'Children?' she finally managed. Vittorio regarded her coolly, waiting. 'You said you needed an heir. How many?'

'Several, if God wills it.' He paused. 'You intimated you wanted children. Will that be a problem?'

'No.' The ache for a baby had only started recently, her biological clock finally having begun its relentless tick. Yet right now she couldn't think of babies, only how they were made.

Her and Vittorio. Her mind danced with images and her body ached with longing. She'd never realized how much desire she could feel, how it caused a sweet, sweet pain to lance through her and leave her breathless with wanting. The knowledge that Vittorio surely did not share it, or at least feel it as she did, that he could talk about the consummation of their marriage—the joining of their bodies— without so much as a flicker of emotion or longing made Ana ache, not just with desire, but with disappointment.

She wished he desired her the way she desired him, a wonderful consuming ache that longed only to be sated. Yes, she knew she could stir him to sensuality, but surely any man—well, *almost* any man—would have such a response.

Was it enough?

'Ana, what are you thinking?' Vittorio asked. His voice was gentle, and Ana saw a wary compassion in his eyes.

'I'm thinking I don't want to marry a man who doesn't find me attractive,' she said flatly. The words seemed to lie heavily between them, unable to be unsaid. Vittorio's face was blank, but Ana sensed his withdrawal, as if he'd actually recoiled from the brutal honesty of her words.

'I think you are being too harsh.'

The fact that he did not deny it completely made

her heart sink a little. 'Am I?' she asked, and heard the hurt in her own voice.

'You felt the evidence of my desire for you the other night,' Vittorio told her in a low voice. A smile lurked in his eyes. 'Didn't you?'

Ana flushed. 'Yes, but—'

'Admittedly, you are different from the other women I've... known. But that doesn't mean I can't find you attractive.'

Having drunk enough whisky and given the right inducements, Ana silently added. 'Have you had many lovers?' she asked impulsively, and almost laughed at Vittorio's expression of utter surprise.

'Enough,' he said after a moment. 'But there is no point raking over either of our pasts, Ana. As I said before, we should look now to the future. Our future.'

Ana tossed her napkin on the table, suddenly restless, needing to move. 'I've finished. Shall we? The last boat back to Fusina leaves before midnight.'

'So it does.' Vittorio raised one hand with easy grace to signal for the bill, and within minutes they were winding their way through the tables and then outside, the spring air slightly damp, the heady scent of flowers mixing with the faint whiff of stagnant water from one of the canals, an aroma that belonged purely to Venice. 'Shall we walk?' Vittorio asked, taking her arm; it fitted snugly into his and her side collided not unpleasantly with his hip. She could feel the hard contours of his leg against hers.

The piazza outside San Marco had emptied of tourists and now only a few people lingered over half-drunk glasses of wine at the pavement cafés; Ana saw a couple entwined in the shadows by one of the pillars of the ancient church. She found herself hurrying, needing to move, to get somewhere. Her thoughts—her hopes, her fears—were too much to deal with.

They didn't speak as they made their way back to the ferry and, even once aboard the boat, they both stood at the rail, silently watching the lights of Venice disappear into the darkness and fog.

Ana knew she should have a thousand questions to ask, a dozen different points to clarify. Her mind buzzed with thoughts, concerns flitting in and out of her scattered brain.

'I don't want my children to be raised by some nanny,' she blurted and Vittorio glanced sideways at her, his hands still curved around the railing of the ferry.

'Of course not.'

'And I refuse to send them to boarding school.' Her two years at a girls' school near Florence had been some of the darkest days she'd ever known. Even now, she suppressed a shudder at the memory. Vittorio's expression didn't even flicker, although she sensed a tension rippling from him, like a current in the air.

'On that point we are of one accord. I did not enjoy

boarding school particularly, and I am presuming you didn't either.'

'No.' She licked her lips; her mouth was suddenly impossibly dry. 'You can't expect to change me.' Vittorio simply arched an eyebrow and waited. 'With make-up and clothes and such. If you wanted that kind of woman, Vittorio, you should have asked someone else.' She met his bland gaze defiantly, daring him to tell her—what? That she needed a little polish? That her shapeless trouser suits—expensive as they were—would have to go? That she wasn't beautiful or glamorous enough for him? Or was that simply what *she* thought?

'There would be little point in attempting to change you,' he finally said, 'when I have asked you to marry me as you are.' Ana nodded jerkily, and then he continued. 'However, you will be the Countess of Cazlevara. I expect you to act—and dress—according to your station.'

'What does that mean exactly?'

Vittorio shrugged. 'You are an intelligent adult woman, Ana. I'll leave such decisions to you.'

Ana nodded, accepting, and they didn't speak until they were off the boat and back in Vittorio's Porsche, speeding through the darkness. A heavy fog rested over the hills above Treviso, lending an eerie glow to the road, the car's headlights barely penetrating the swirling mist. The air was chilly and damp and Ana's mind flitted immediately to the vineyards, the grapes still young and fragile. She didn't think it was cold enough to be concerned and she leaned her head back against the seat, suddenly overwhelmingly exhausted.

Vittorio turned into Villa Rosso's sweeping drive, parking the car in front of the villa's front doors and killing the engine. The world seemed impossibly silent, and Ana felt as if she could nearly fall asleep right there in the car.

'Go to bed, *rondinella*,' Vittorio said softly. His thumb skimmed her cheek, pressed lightly on her chin. 'Sleep on it awhile.'

Ana's eyes fluttered open, his words penetrating her fogged mind slowly. 'What did you say?' she asked in a whisper.

Vittorio's mouth curved in a small smile, yet Ana saw a shadow of sorrow in his eyes, lit only by the lights of the villa and the moon, which had escaped from the clouds that longed to hide it from view. 'I told you to sleep. And preferably in a bed, I think.'

'Yes, but—' Ana swallowed and struggled to a more upright position. 'What did you call me?'

'*Rondinella.*' His smile deepened, as did the sorrow in his eyes. 'You think I don't remember?'

Ana stared at him, her eyes wide, thoughts and realizations tumbling through her now-clear mind. He remembered. Suddenly she was back at her mother's graveside, her hand still caked with mud, tears drying on her cheeks. Suddenly she was looking at the only person who had shown her true compassion;

even her own father had been too dazed by grief to deal with his daughter. And suddenly the answer was obvious.

'I don't need to sleep on it,' she said, her words no more than a breath of sound.

Hope lit Vittorio's eyes, replacing the sorrow. His smile seemed genuine now and he touched her cheek again with his thumb. 'You don't?'

'No.' She reached up to clasp his hand with her own, her fingers curling around his. 'The answer is yes, Vittorio. I'll marry you.'

CHAPTER SIX

EVERYTHING happened quickly after that. It was as if her acceptance had set off a chain reaction of events, spurring Vittorio into purposeful action that left Ana breathless and a little uncertain. It was all happening so *fast*.

The morning after she'd accepted his proposal—his proposition—he came to the winery offices. Seeing him there, looking official and elegant in his dark grey suit, the only colour the crimson silk of his tie, Ana was reminded just how businesslike this marriage really was. Vittorio hardly seemed the same man who had caressed her cheek and called her swallow only the evening before. The memory of his touch still lingered in her mind, tingled her nerve-endings.

'I thought we should go over some details,' Vittorio said now. 'If you have time?'

Ana braced her hands on her desk, nodding with swift purpose, an attempt to match Vittorio's own brisk determination. 'Of course.' He paused, and Ana moved from behind the desk. 'Why don't we adjourn to the wine-tasting room? I'll order coffee.'

He smiled then, seeming pleased with her suggestion. Just another business meeting, Ana thought a bit sourly, even as she reprimanded herself that she had no right to be resentful of Vittorio's businesslike attitude. She was meant to share it.

Once they were seated on the leather sofas in the wine-tasting room, a tray of coffee on the table between them, Vittorio took out a paper that, to Ana, looked like a laundry list. He withdrew a pair of wire-rimmed spectacles and perched them on the end of his nose, making an unexpected bubble of laughter rise up her throat and escape in a gurgle of sound. 'I didn't know you wore specs.'

He arched his eyebrows, smiling ruefully. 'I started needing them when I turned thirty-five, alas.'

'Is that in your medical file?' Ana couldn't help but quip. 'I should have a full report, you know.'

'I'll have it sent to you immediately,' Vittorio returned, and Ana realized she didn't know if he was joking or not. To cover her confusion she busied herself with preparing the coffee.

'I realize I don't know how old you are,' she commented lightly. 'At my mother's funeral, you were— what? Twenty?'

'Twenty-one.'

The mood suddenly turned sober, dark with memories. Ana gazed at him over the rim of her coffee cup. 'Your father died when you were around my age then, didn't he?'

'Yes. I was fourteen.'

'A heart attack, wasn't it? Sudden.'

Vittorio nodded. 'Yes, as was your mother's death, if I remember correctly. A car accident?'

Ana nodded. 'A drunk driver. A boy no more than seventeen.' She shook her head in sorrowful memory. 'He lost his life as well.'

'I always felt like the death of a parent skewed the world somehow,' Vittorio said after a moment. 'No matter how happy you are, nothing seems quite right after that.' Ana nodded jerkily; he'd expressed it perfectly. He understood. Vittorio looked away, sipping his coffee before he cleared his throat and consulted his list. 'I thought we could have a quiet ceremony in the chapel at Castle Cazlevara. Unless you object?'

'No, of course not. That sounds…fine.'

'If you envisioned something else—'

'No.' She'd stopped dreaming of any kind of wedding years ago. The thought of a huge spectacle now seemed like an affront, a travesty, considering the true nature of their marriage. The thought was an uncomfortable one. 'A quiet ceremony will be fine,' she said a bit flatly, and Vittorio frowned.

'As long as you are sure.' He turned back to his list, a frown still wrinkling his forehead, drawing those strong, straight brows closer together. 'As for dates, I thought in two weeks' time.'

Ana nearly spluttered her mouthful of coffee. 'Two *weeks*!'

'Three, then, at the most. There is no reason to wait, is there?'

'No, I suppose not,' Ana agreed reluctantly. 'Still, won't it seem…odd? People might talk.'

'I am not interested in gossip. In any case, the sooner we marry, the sooner we become…used to one another.' He gave her the glimmer of a smile. 'Of course, we can wait—a while—before we consummate the marriage. I want you to feel comfortable.'

Ana blushed. She couldn't help it. Despite his tone of cool, clinical detachment, she could imagine that consummation so vividly. Wonderfully. And she didn't want to wait. She took another sip of coffee, hiding her face from Vittorio's knowing gaze. She wasn't about to admit as much, not when Vittorio was all too content to delay the event.

'Thank you for that sensitivity,' she murmured after a moment, and Vittorio nodded and returned to his list.

'I thought a small wedding, but do let me know if there is anyone in particular you would like to invite.'

'I'll have to think about it.'

'I realize if we invited only some of the local winemakers, others will be insulted at not being included,' Vittorio continued. 'So I thought not to invite any… We'll have a party at the castle a few days after the wedding. Everyone can come then.'

'All right.' Ana wished she could contribute something more coherent to this conversation other than her mindless murmured agreements. Yet she couldn't; her mind was spinning with these new developments, realizations. Implications.

In a short while—as little as two weeks—they could be married. *Would* be married. Her hand trembled and she put the coffee cup back in its saucer with an inelegant clatter.

'We will need witnesses, of course, for the ceremony,' Vittorio said, reaching for his own cup. If he noticed Ana's agitation, he did not remark on it. 'Is there a woman friend in particular you would like to stand witness?'

'Yes, a friend from university.' Paola was still her best friend, although they saw each other infrequently ever since her friend had married a Sicilian. She'd moved south and had babies. Ana had moved home, caring for her father and the winery. 'She'll be surprised,' Ana said a bit wryly. She could only imagine Paola's shock when she told her she was getting married, and so suddenly. 'And what about you? Who will you have as your witness?'

'I thought your father.'

'My father!' Ana couldn't keep the surprise from her voice; she didn't even try. 'But…'

'He is a good man.'

'What about your brother?'

'No.' Vittorio's voice was flat and when his gaze met Ana's his eyes looked hard, even unfriendly. 'We are not close.'

There was a world of knowledge in that statement, Ana knew, a lifetime of memory and perhaps regret. She longed to ask why—what—but she knew now was not the time. 'Very well.'

Vittorio finished his coffee and folded his list back into his breast pocket. 'I assume I can leave the details of your dress and flowers to you?' he asked. His eyebrow arched, a hint of a smile around his mouth, he added, 'You will wear a dress?'

Ana managed a smile back. 'Yes. For my own wedding, I think I can manage a dress.'

'Good. Then I'll leave you to work now. I thought you could come to dinner this Friday, at the castle. You will need to meet my family.' Again that hardness, that darkness.

Ana nodded. 'Yes, of course.'

And then he was gone. He rose from the table, shook her hand and left the office as if it had just been another business meeting, which, Ana recognized, of course it had.

That evening, over dinner, she told her father. She could have told him that morning, but something had held her back. Perhaps it was her own reluctance to admit she'd done something that seemed so foolhardy, so desperate. Yet, now the wedding was a mere fortnight away, she could hardly keep such

news from her father, especially if Vittorio intended
for him to stand as witness.

'I said yes to Vittorio, Papà,' Ana said as they finished the soup course. Her voice came out sounding
rather flat.

Enrico lowered his spoon, his eyes widening in
surprise, a smile blooming across his dear wrinkled
face. 'But Ana! *Dolcezza!* That is wonderful.'

'I hope it will be,' Ana allowed, and Enrico
nodded in understanding.

'You are nervous? Afraid?'

'A bit.'

'He is a good man.'

'I'm glad you think so.'

Enrico cocked his head. 'You aren't sure?'

Ana considered this. 'I would hardly marry a bad
man, Papà.' Vittorio was a good man, she knew.
Honourable, just, moral. She thought of that hardness
in his eyes and voice when he spoke of his family.
He was a good man, but was he a gentle man? Then
she remembered the whisper of his thumb on her
cheek, the soft words of comfort. *It's all right...
rondinella.*

She didn't know what to think. What to believe
or even to hope for.

'I am happy for you,' Enrico said, reaching over to
cover her hand with his own. 'For you both. When
is the wedding?'

Ana swallowed. 'In two weeks.'

Enrico raised his eyebrows. 'Good,' he said after

a moment. 'No need to waste time. I will telephone Aunt Iris today. Perhaps she can come from England.'

Ana nodded jerkily. She'd only met her aunt a handful of times; she'd disapproved of her sister marrying an Italian and living so far away. When Emily had died, she'd withdrawn even more. 'I hope she'll come,' Ana said, meaning it. Perhaps her wedding could go some way towards healing such family rifts.

Even when at work in the winery on Monday she found her thoughts were too hopelessly scattered to concentrate on much of anything. She jumped at the littlest sound, half-expecting, hoping even, to see Vittorio again. He did not make an appearance.

In the middle of a task or phone call she would catch herself staring into space, her mind leaping ahead...*I'll be the Countess of Cazlevara. What will people say? When will Vittorio want to—?*

She forced her mind back to her work, even as a lump of something—half dread, half excitement— lodged in her middle and made it impossible to eat or even to swallow more than a sip of water. She was a seething mass of nerves, wondering just what insane foolishness she'd agreed to, longing to possess the cool business sense Vittorio had credited her with. She couldn't summon it for the life of her.

On Thursday evening, as she headed back to the villa, she compiled a list in her head of all the things she needed to do. Tell the winery staff. Ring Paola. Find an outfit—a dress?—for her dinner with Vittorio and his family tomorrow.

The downstairs of the villa was quiet and dark when Ana entered.

'Papà?' she called, and there was no answer. She headed upstairs, pausing in the doorway of one of the guest bedrooms they never used. Her father, she saw, was seated on the floor, his head bowed. Ana felt a lurch of alarm. 'Papa?' she asked gently. 'Are you all right?'

He looked up, blinking once or twice, and smiled brightly. 'Yes. Fine. I was just looking through some old things.'

Ana stepped into the room, now lost in the gloom of late afternoon. 'What old things?' she asked.

'Of your mother's…' The words trailed off in a sigh. Enrico looked down at his lap, which was covered by a heap of crumpled white satin. 'She would be so pleased to know you were getting married. I like to think that she does know, somehow. Somewhere.'

'Yes.' Ana couldn't help but remember Vittorio's words: *tua cuore.* 'What's that on your lap?'

'Your mother's wedding dress. Have I never shown it to you?'

Ana shook her head. 'In photographs…'

Enrico held it up, shaking it out as he smiled tremulously. 'I know it's probably out-of-date,' he began, his voice hesitant. 'And it needs to be professionally cleaned and most likely altered, but…'

'But?' Ana prompted. She felt moved by her father's obvious emotion—unusual as it was—but it saddened her too. This enduring love was something she'd agreed never to know.

'It would give this old man great joy for you to wear your mother's gown on your wedding day,' Enrico said, and Ana's heart sank a little bit.

'You're not an old man, Papà,' she protested, even as she scanned his face, noticing how thin and white his hair was, the new deeper grooves on the sides of his mouth. He'd been forty when he'd married; he was just past seventy now. It seemed impossible, and her heart lurched as she reached for the gown. 'Let me see.' She shook the dress out, admiring the rich white satin even as she recognized the style—over thirty years old—was far from flattering for her own fuller figure. The round neckline was bedecked with heavy lace and the skirt had three tiers of ruffles. Not only would she look like a meringue in it, she would look like a very large meringue. She'd look *awful*. Ana turned back to her father; tears shimmered in his eyes. She smiled. 'I'd be honoured to wear it, Papà.'

The next day Ana stood outside Castle Cazlevara. The torches guttered in a chilly spring breeze and lights twinkled from within. Even before she stepped out of her car—she'd insisted on driving herself—a liveried footman threw open the double doors and welcomed her inside.

'Signorina Viale, welcome. The Count and his mother, the Countess, are in the drawing room awaiting your arrival.'

Ana swallowed past the dryness in her mouth; her heart had begun to thump so loudly she could feel it in her ears. She straightened, her hands running down the silvery-grey wide-legged trousers she wore. She'd taken great pains over her outfit, and yet now she wondered if it was as plain as the other trouser suits she donned as armour. Only yesterday she'd taken the ferry to Venice, had even ventured down Frezzeria to the chic boutique Vittorio had led her to just the other night. She'd stood in front of the window like a child in front of a sweet shop; twice she'd almost gone in. But the stick-thin sales associate with her black pencil skirt and crisp white blouse looked so svelte and elegant and forbidding that after twenty minutes Ana had crept away. The thought of trying on such beautiful clothes—of looking at herself in such beautiful clothes—in front of such a woman was too intimidating. Too terrifying.

So she'd scoured her closet, finding a pair of trousers she'd never worn; the fabric shimmered as she moved and even though it was still a pair of trousers, the legs were wide enough to almost pass for a skirt. She chose the beaded top she'd worn the last time she'd come to the castle and she'd pulled back her hair loosely so a few loose tendrils framed her face, softening the effect. She'd even put on a little lipstick.

Now as she made her way to the drawing room, she wondered if Vittorio would notice. If he would care. And, if he did, would she be glad? She couldn't decide if she would feel more of a fool if he did notice or if he didn't.

All these thoughts flew from her head as she stood in the doorway of the drawing room and a slim, petite blonde—the kind of woman who made Ana feel like an ungainly giant—swivelled to face her. Constantia Ralfino, the Countess of Cazlevara. Soon to be the *Dowager* Countess.

The moment seemed suspended in time as they both stood there, the Countess taking in Ana with one arctic sweep of her eyes. Ana quailed under that gaze; she felt herself shrivel inside, for Constantia Cazlevara was looking at her as so many people had looked at her, beginning with most of the girls at the boarding school her father had sent her to after her mother had died.

It was a look of assessment and then disdain, followed swiftly by dismissal. It was a look that hurt now, more than it should, because it made Ana feel like a gawky thirteen-year-old again, awkward and still stricken with grief.

'So,' Constantia said coolly. She lifted her chin and met Ana's humble gaze directly. 'This is your bride.'

Her tone was most likely meant to be neutral, but Ana heard contempt. She lifted her chin as well.

'Yes. We met many years ago, my lady. Of course, I am pleased to make your acquaintance once more.'

'Indeed.' Constantia did not make any move to take Ana's proffered hand, and after a moment she dropped it. Constantia turned to Vittorio, who was watching them both in tight-lipped silence. 'Aren't you going to introduce us, Vittorio?'

'Ana seems to have accomplished the introductions better than I ever could,' he said in a clipped voice. 'However, if you must.' He waved one hand between the pair of them. 'Mother, this is Ana Viale, one of the region's most promising winemakers, daughter of our neighbour Enrico Viale, and my intended bride.' His lips, once pursed so tightly, now curved in a smile that still managed to seem unpleasant. 'Ana, this is my mother, Constantia.'

The tension almost made the air shiver; Ana imagined she could hear it crackle. Constantia shot her son a look of barely veiled resentment before she turned back to Ana. 'So was it love at first sight, my dear?'

Ana couldn't tell if the older woman was baiting her or genuinely interested in knowing. She glanced at Vittorio, wondering what to say. How to dissemble. Did he want people to know just how convenient their marriage was meant to be? Or was he intending to deceive everyone into thinking they were in love?

Such a charade would be exhausting and ultimately pointless, Ana was sure.

Before she could frame an answer, Vittorio cut in. 'Love at first sight? What a question, Mother. Ana and I both know there is no such thing. Now, dinner is served and I don't enjoy eating it cold. Let's withdraw to the dining room.' He strode from the room, pausing only to offer Ana his arm, which she accepted awkwardly, her elbow crooked in his, her strides made awkwardly longer than normal in order to match his.

Dinner was, of course, interminable. Vittorio and Constantia both spoke with that chilly politeness that managed to be worse than outright barbs or even insults. Ana felt her whole body tense and she had the beginnings of a terrible headache. It was impossible to know what to say, how to act. Vittorio gave her no clues.

A thousand questions and, worse, doubts, whirled in her head, demanding answers. What was the source of the antipathy between Vittorio and his mother? How could two people in the same family seem to dislike each other so much? And how could she possibly fit into this unhappy picture? The thought of living in Castle Cazlevara with Constantia's continual scorn and disdain was unendurable. An hour into the evening, Ana was just beginning to realize how much she'd agreed to when she'd accepted Vittorio's proposal. Not just a marriage, but a family. Not just a business proposition, but a lifestyle. A *life*.

She felt fraught with nerves, sick with dread by the time the miserable meal came to an end. There had been some sort of conversation, she supposed, desultory remarks that still managed to be pointed, poised to wound. Ana had contributed very little; she'd eaten less, merely toying with her food.

Constantia rose from the table in one graceful movement. She was a slender slip of a woman, still strikingly beautiful despite the wrinkles that lined her face like a piece of parchment that had been crumpled up and smoothed out again. 'I'm afraid I'm too weary from my journey to stay for coffee,' she said, offering Ana a cool little smile. 'I do hope you'll forgive me, my dear.'

'Of course,' Ana murmured. She was relieved to be able to avoid any further awkwardness with her future mother-in-law—if she was even going to marry Vittorio. A single evening had cast everything into terrible doubt.

'Well, then.' She turned to Vittorio, her haughty expression seeming to turn sad, the cool little smile softening into something that looked weary and lost. Before Ana could even register what that look meant, it had cleared, leaving Constantia distant and regal once more, and with one last haughty look she swept from the room and left Vittorio and Ana suspended in a tense and uneasy silence.

'Vittorio—' Ana began, the word bursting from

her. She stopped, unable to continue, afraid to frame the thoughts pounding through her head.

'What is it, Ana?' His tone was sharp, his look assessing. Knowing. 'You're not having second thoughts already?' he asked, his voice soft now and yet still faintly menacing. He rose from the table, coming around to help Ana from her chair. His hands slid down her bare shoulders in what was surely no more than a pretext to touch her; she shivered noticeably. 'Cold feet, *rondinella*?' he whispered and she shook her head, sudden pain lancing through her.

'Don't call me that.'

'Why not?'

'Because—' She pressed her lips together. It would sound foolish—pathetic, even—to admit the endearment was special. That it *meant* something. Yet still she couldn't stand Vittorio using it now, when his expression was so forbidding, his voice faintly mocking. When there suddenly seemed so much she didn't know about him, so much she was afraid of.

'Because why?' Vittorio asked. He'd trailed his hand down Ana's bare arm so now their fingertips were touching. Smiling faintly, he laced his fingers with her own and drew her from the table, out into the foyer with its flickering torches, the ancient stones dancing with shadows. 'We are about to be married, after all.'

Ana let him lead her. His touch was mesmerizing, her thoughts and even doubts seeming to fly from

her head as she followed him slowly, knowing each
step was taking her closer to danger. Danger, and
yet such exquisite danger it was. All she could think
or feel was his fingers on her skin. Wanting more.
Needing more.

'I don't—' she began, and then simply shook her
head, at a loss for words. Feeling was too much,
taking over every sense.

'You don't…?' Vittorio prompted. She thought she
heard laughter in his voice; he *knew*. He knew how
much his simple touch affected her, reduced her. He
used it as a weapon. His fingers still laced with hers,
he pulled her towards him. She came, unresisting,
until their bodies collided and she had to tilt back her
head to look up into his face, his onyx eyes glittering
as he gazed down at her. 'Don't be afraid, Ana,' he
murmured, his lips inches from hers.

Her own lips parted instinctively, yet also in anticipation. *Hope.* Even so, she summoned one last
protest; it was both an attack and a defence. 'There's
so much I don't know about you, Vittorio.'

'Mmm.' Vittorio's fingers trailed up and down
her arm, playing her skin like an instrument, his lips
now a scant inch from hers so his breath feathered
her face. She knew what he was doing. He was dis-
tracting her, keeping her from asking the questions
whose answers she needed to know, whose answers,
she realized fuzzily, might keep her from marrying
him. And, even as she knew this, she couldn't help

her overwhelming response to his touch, blocking out all rational thought, all sense of reason.

And so another damning thought followed on the heels of the first: that *nothing* could keep her from marrying Vittorio, from possessing him, or having him possess her. She knew that as, with his free hand, he cupped her cheek and brought her face closer to his, their lips now no more than a breath apart.

He was going to kiss her. She needed him to kiss her, craved it, knew that her body and mind and soul could not be satisfied until she'd felt his lips on hers once more. Later, she knew, she would be humbled and perhaps ashamed by her own helpless desire. For now, it remained only an unstoppable force, an overwhelming hunger. So much so, in fact, that in barely a breath of sound, she whispered, *begged*, 'Kiss me.'

Vittorio's mouth curved in a smile tinged with triumph. Ana didn't care. She didn't care if she was humiliating herself, if Vittorio would gloat in his sensual power over her. She *couldn't* care, because the need was too strong. 'Kiss me,' she said again, and then, because still he just smiled, she closed the gap between their lips herself, her eyes closing in blissful relief as their mouths connected and her whole body flooded with both satisfaction and yet more need.

Her hands found their way to his hair, fisting in its softness, her body pressing against the full length of his. She let her mouth move slowly over his, let her tongue slide against his lips, knowing she was inexpert, clumsy even, and not caring because it felt so good. She lost herself in that kiss, sank into it like she would a big feather bed, revelling in its softness, its wonder and pleasure, until she realized—slowly— that Vittorio had not moved, had not responded at all. Dimly, distantly, she became aware that his body was rigid against hers, his hands only loosely on her shoulders, his lips unresponsive and even slack under hers.

Desire had swamped her senses, flooded her reason, and yet Vittorio barely seemed affected at all.

In a sickening flash she remembered how she'd kissed Roberto—just as clumsily, no doubt—and how he had not moved either. He had remained still, enduring her touch, relieved when it was over. He'd felt disgust, not desire. And—oh, please, no—was Vittorio the same? She took a stumbling step backwards, shame pouring through her, scalding her senses, making her eager for escape.

Yet Vittorio would not let her flee. His hands came up to encircle her arms and he pulled her towards him as he deepened the kiss and made it his own. His hands moved to her hips, rocking her so their bodies collided in the most intimate way, and her lips curved in a triumphant, incredulous smile when she heard his sharp intake of breath and felt the evidence of his arousal.

Yet if Ana felt she was in control—even for a second—she soon realized she was sorely mistaken. Vittorio had taken command, pulling her into even closer contact, keeping her there, trapped between his powerful thighs. His mouth, at first so still and unresponsive under hers, now moved with deliberate, languorous ease, travelling from her lips to the sensitive skin under her ear so she was the one gasping aloud, and then to the intimate curve of her neck, and finally to the vee between her breasts.

Ana threw her head back, her eyes clenched shut, her breath coming in audible moans. She'd never been touched so intimately, so *much*. Her head spun and her body felt as if every nerve-ending had blazed to life; it almost hurt to feel this much, to know such pleasure.

She'd never known that *anything* could be like this.

Then Vittorio stepped away, leaving Ana reeling and gasping, the aftershocks of exquisite sensation still rocking her, and he smiled rather coolly. 'See, Ana?' he said, reaching behind her to open the front door of the castle; a cool breeze blew over her heated body. 'I think you know me well enough.'

Vittorio waited until Ana was safely in her car, making her way down the curving drive, before he let out a long, low shudder.

He had not expected that. He'd been planning to seduce Ana, to sweep away her doubts with a kiss—or two. Instead, *she'd* kissed *him*. He'd been shocked by her audacity as well as his response. For, in that kiss, he'd realized that Ana was more than this thing he wanted, this possession he meant to acquire, his goal achieved. *Wife.*

She was a person, a being with hopes and needs and oh, yes, desires—and, even as he'd sent his little gifts and said the right words and kissed her, he'd somehow managed to forget this fact. Had he ever really known it?

Why he should realize that when she'd been kissing him, pressing against him, stirring him to a sudden desperate lust, he had no idea. He wished he hadn't realized; it was easier not to know, or at least to pretend not to know.

To hold someone's happiness in your hand, to take responsibility for her life—

It was monumental. Frightening, too.

'Why, Vittorio?'

Vittorio stilled, his mother's accusing voice ringing in his ears. He turned slowly, his gaze sweeping over her in one dismissive glance. She stood poised on the bottom step of the ornate marble staircase—a nineteenth-century addition to the castle—her eyes blazing blue fire and her mouth twisted into a contemptuous sneer. It was an expression he'd become accustomed to.

'Why what, Mother?' he asked, his words holding only a veneer of icy politeness.

'Why are you marrying that poor girl?'

Vittorio's eyes narrowed. 'I don't appreciate the way you refer to my bride. There is nothing poor about Ana.'

Constantia let out a crow of disbelieving laughter. 'Come, Vittorio! I know the women you've taken to your bed. I've seen them in the tabloids. They would eat Anamaria Viale alive.'

He just kept himself from flinching. 'They will never have the opportunity.'

'No?' Constantia took a step towards him, incredulity lacing the single word. 'You think not? And how will you manage that, my son? Will you keep your precious wife locked away in a glass case? Because, I assure you, that is not a pleasant place to be.'

'I have no intention of putting Ana anywhere,' Vittorio said flatly, 'that she does not wish to be.'

'She loves you,' Constantia said after a moment. Her voice was quiet. 'Or at least she could.'

Vittorio's jaw tightened. 'That is no concern of yours, Mother.'

'Isn't it?' Constantia lifted her chin, her expression challenging and obdurate. 'Do you know how it feels to love someone and never have them love you back? Do you know what that can drive you to think, to *do*?' Her voice rang out, raw and ragged, and Vittorio narrowed his eyes. Her words—her tone—made no sense to him; was her obvious distress another ploy?

'What are you talking about?'

Constantia pressed her lips together and shook her head. 'Why are you going to marry her, Vittorio? Is it simply to spite me?'

'You give yourself too much credit.'

'You had no interest in marriage until I spoke of it.'

Vittorio lifted one shoulder in a careless shrug. 'You simply reminded me to do my duty as Count of Cazlevara and CEO of Cazlevara Wines,' he said. 'It is my duty to provide an heir.'

'So Bernardo cannot take your place,' she finished flatly.

Vittorio's eyes narrowed. She didn't even hide her true ambition, but then she never had. 'Every man wants a son.'

'Why her?' Constantia demanded. 'Why marry a woman you could not love?'

'I'm not interested in love, Mother.'

'Just like your father, then,' she spat, and again Vittorio felt a confused lurch of unease which he forced himself to dismiss.

'I'm finished with this conversation,' he said shortly and he turned away, walking quickly from the room. It was only later, when he was preparing for bed, that he remembered and reflected on his mother's words. She'd called Ana a woman he could not love, as if such a thing—to love Ana—was an impossibility.

His hands stilling on the buttons of his shirt,

Vittorio wondered if his mother spoke the truth. He'd never *wanted* to love, that was true; was he even capable of it?

CHAPTER SEVEN

TODAY was her wedding day. Ana stared at her reflection in her bedroom mirror and grimaced. She looked awful. Although she couldn't regret the decision to wear her mother's wedding gown, neither could she suppress the natural longing to look better in it.

The gown had been professionally cleaned and altered, but it was still befrilled and belaced to within an inch of its life—and hers. The thought of Vittorio seeing her looking like Little Bo Beep from a bad pantomime made her cringe. Sighing, she stroked the rich satin—no matter what the style, the dress was of the highest quality—and forced such negative thoughts from her mind. Today was her wedding day. She wanted to enjoy it.

Yet other negative thoughts—the doubts and fears that had dogged her since her dinner with Vittorio and Constantia—crept in and gnawed at her already struggling sense of happiness.

She'd seen Vittorio many times in the last fortnight; he'd made a point of stopping by the winery office, whether it was for a simple hello, or to show her a magazine article on the latest growing techniques, or to stroll through the Viale vineyards with her, the sun blazing benevolently down on them as they walked. Ana appreciated his attempts to make their relationship at least appear normal and pleasant, yet she couldn't quite stop the creeping doubt that, even though she enjoyed them, the visits seemed a little…*perfunctory*. Another item ticked off on her husband-to-be's to-do list. He'd acquired his bride; now he was maintaining her.

She knew she shouldn't begrudge Vittorio the time he spent with her, and she shouldn't expect more. She shouldn't even *want* more. She'd agreed to a business-minded marriage, she reminded herself, not nearly for the first time. She had to stick to her side of the bargain.

Someone tapped on the door and then a dark curly head peeked round the frame. 'Are you ready?' Paola asked. Ever since Ana had told her friend about her upcoming wedding, Paola had been wonderfully supportive. Ana had not yet told her the truth of her marriage. 'The car is here to take you to the castle.'

Ana nodded. 'Yes, I just need my veil.'

Smiling, Paola reached for the gossamer-thin veil of webbed lace and settled it on Ana's head. She wore her hair up in a chignon, clusters of curls at the corners of her brow. 'You look…' Paola began, and Ana smiled wryly.

'Terrible.'

Paola smiled back at Ana, their eyes meeting in the mirror. 'I wasn't going to say that.'

'The dress doesn't suit me in the least.'

Paola gave a little shrug. 'I think it's wonderful you're wearing your mother's gown and anyone with any sense will think the same, no matter what it looks like. Anyway,' she continued robustly as she twitched the veil so the lace flowed down Ana's back, 'I think a bride could wear a bin bag and it wouldn't matter at all. When you're in love, you glow. No one looks better than a bride on her wedding day.'

'You think so?' Ana asked, her voice pitched just a little too shrill. She didn't glow, and it was no wonder. She wasn't in love. She looked, in fact, rather pasty.

Paola laid a hand on Ana's shoulder. 'Is everything all right, Ana? I know we haven't been in touch in a while, but—' she paused, chewing her lip '—you seem so nervous. Everyone has cold feet, of course. I was nearly sick the morning of my own wedding, do you remember? But…are you sure this is what you want?' She softened the question with a smile, adding, 'It's my duty as your bridesmaid and witness to ask that, you know.'

'I know.' Ana made herself smile back, despite the nerves that were fluttering rather madly in her stomach and threatening to make their way up her throat. 'Yes, Paola, this is what I want.' No matter how nervous she was now, Ana knew she couldn't go back to her old life, her old ways. She couldn't walk out on Vittorio, and what marriage to him would—could—mean. She let out her breath slowly. 'If I seem particularly nervous, it's because this marriage isn't—isn't really a normal marriage.'

Paola frowned. 'What are you talking about?'

'Vittorio and I only agreed to get married a fortnight ago,' Ana explained in a rush. She felt better for admitting the truth she hadn't been brave enough to reveal since Paola's arrival two days ago. 'We're not in love, not even close. It's a marriage...of convenience.'

'Convenience?' Paola echoed. She gave a disbelieving laugh. 'Just what is convenient about marriage?'

Ana tried for a laugh as well; the sound came out shaky. 'Vittorio and I have common goals. We're both ambitious and we have similar ideas about... things...' She trailed off, realizing how absurd she sounded. She didn't even know if she believed half of what she said. From the look in Paola's narrowed eyes, neither did her friend.

'Ana, are you really sure—'

A knock sounded at the door and the muffled voice of her father could be heard from behind it. 'Ana, *dolcezza*, are you ready? The car is here and if we are to be on time...'

Ana took a deep breath. Her wedding day was here; the moment had arrived. In less than an hour she would be married to Vittorio, she would be

the Countess of Cazlevara. A thousand thoughts
and memories flitted through her dazed mind: the
moment when she'd learned her mother had died,
and her whole world fell away. Her father's refusal even to see her, hiding his grief behind locked
doors, insisting she attend boarding school. The
hellish days at that school, alone, grief-stricken,
awkward and miserable, teased and ignored. Then,
later, her years at university, slowly learning how
to be confident, what it would take to be success-
ful, only to have her frail self-esteem obliterated by
that awful moment in Roberto's arms. The nights
spent gazing out of her window, wondering if life
would ever offer more, if love could be found. The
decision to stop looking for love and enjoy what she
already had, to live for what life offered her rather
than seeking more, always more… All of it, every
second, it seemed then, had led up to this moment
and her decision to marry Vittorio.

And then new, fresh memories raced through her:
the gentle touch of Vittorio's hand on her cheek,
both when she was thirteen and when she was
nearly thirty. The feel of his lips on hers, his hands
on her body, so deft, so desirable. The kindnesses
he'd shown her in the last fortnight—calculated,
perhaps—whether it was a spray of new grapes
or the offer of a new gown. The tension with his
mother, the hope they both had for the future.

And then, to her surprise, as the memories faded
and she blinked the room back into focus, she

realized she was no longer afraid. Her nerves had fled and in their place a new, serene determination had emerged. She smiled at Paola.

'This is what I want, Paola. I am sure.' Turning, Ana called to her father, 'Papà! I'm ready.'

As she opened the door, Enrico blinked tears from his eyes as he saw her in her mother's gown. 'Oh, *dolcezza! Magnifica!*'

Ana smiled.

She didn't quite manage a smile as she saw Vittorio's expression when she came down the aisle of the chapel attached to Castle Cazlevara. Only a dozen guests were scattered among the dark wood pews, a few relatives and friends. Paola, Vittorio and her father all stood at the front as Ana walked down the aisle alone in her mother's ruffled gown.

Vittorio, for a single second, looked horrified. Then his expression smoothed out as if an iron had been applied to it and he gave her the barest flicker of a smile; his eyes remained dark. Ana remembered what she'd once said about her own fashion sense and knew Vittorio was doubting her now. He was probably wondering just what kind of woman he was marrying, when she came down the aisle in a gown thirty years out of date, a gown that made her look like a melting meringue.

Ana lifted her chin and found her smile.

The ceremony only lasted a few minutes, or so

it seemed, for, after a blur of words and motions, Vittorio was sliding the heavy band of antique gold on her finger and then his lips, cool and somehow remote, were pressing her cheek in the chastest of kisses. Even so, Ana's blood stirred and desire leapt low in her belly.

Vittorio stepped away.

Ana heard a spattering of applause from the paltry crowd as if from a great distance, and then Vittorio was leading her down the aisle, away from the chapel and towards the great hall of the castle where their wedding feast would be held.

She sneaked a glance at his profile; his jaw was tight, his gaze staring straight ahead. Ana realized afresh just how much of a stranger her husband was.

Her husband. The thought was incredible, bizarre, ridiculous. Exciting. She swallowed past the fear and remembered her earlier certainty, tried to feel it again.

A servant opened the doors to the great hall, the long table now laid for a meal for twenty. Vittorio turned to her.

'A small wedding reception, and then we can retire. I'm sure you're tired.' He spoke with a careful politeness that managed to make Ana feel even more awkward and strange. She nodded jerkily.

'Thank you.'

Vittorio nodded back, and Ana wondered if this

kind of stilted conversation was what she had to look forward to for the rest of her life.

What had she just done? What had she agreed to?

Like the ceremony, the wedding reception passed in a blur that still managed to make Ana both uncomfortable and exhausted. It wasn't a normal marriage, and people seemed to sense that, so it wasn't a normal wedding reception either. Her friends regarded her a bit quizzically; everyone she'd told had been utterly surprised by her abrupt engagement, although too polite perhaps to show it. Even her Aunt Iris, a distant stranger, scrutinized her with pursed lips and narrowed eyes, as if she suspected that something was amiss. Vittorio's brother, Bernardo, shook her hand; his fingers were cold against hers and his smile didn't reach his eyes. Constantia didn't speak to her at all.

Ana did her best to chat and smile with those who did want to talk to her; she ate a few mouthfuls of the delicious *cicchetti*, meatballs and fried crab, as well as one of the region's specialities, a lobster risotto. And of course there was wine: a rich red wine with the pasta, and crisp white wine with the fish, and prosecco with lemon sorbet for dessert.

By the time the plates had been cleared, Ana felt both exhausted and a bit dizzy. She saw Vittorio signal to a servant, and then moments later felt someone's hand on her shoulder. She turned and saw Paola smiling at her.

'Come, the wedding feast is nearly over. I'll help you out of your dress.'

'Out of…?' Ana repeated blankly, her mind fuzzy from the food and wine. Of course; the wedding was over, it was now her wedding night.

Vittorio had been vague about what he expected—what he *wanted*—from their first night together as husband and wife. He'd mentioned that he would give her time; there was no need to consummate their marriage on the very first night.

Yet what did he want? What did she want?

She knew the answer to the second question: *him.*

Ana let Paola lead her away from the reception, up to an unfamiliar corridor—she'd never even been upstairs before—and finally to a bedroom suite. Ana took in the massive stone fireplace, a fire already laid, the huge four poster bed piled high with velvet and satin pillows and the dimmed lighting. It was a room for seduction. It was a room for love.

'How did you know where to go?' she asked Paola, who had already closed the door and was reaching for the back of Ana's dress, and the thirty-six buttons that went from the nape of her neck to the small of her back.

'One of the servants showed me. Vittorio has a timetable, apparently. It's all very organized, isn't it?'

'That's a good thing,' Ana replied. She couldn't

help but feel just a little defensive; she heard a note of censure in her friend's voice.

'So,' Paola asked as she finished with the buttons and the dress sank around Ana's ankles in a pool of satin, 'just how convenient is this marriage, anyway?' She gestured towards the room with its candlelight and pillows with a wry smile.

'Not that convenient, I suppose.' Ana smiled, felt the leap of anticipation in her belly, the tightening of her muscles and nerves in heady expectation. She was ready. She *wanted* this. So terribly, dangerously much.

'Do you love him, Ana?' Paola asked quietly. Ana stepped out of her dress, standing in just a thin slip, and reached for the pins that held her hair in its fussy chignon. Her back remained to Paola.

'No,' she said after a moment, 'but that's all right.'

'Is it?'

Ana turned around. 'I know you married for love, Paola, but that doesn't mean it's the only way. Vittorio and I want to be happy together, and I think we will be.' Brave words. She'd believed them once, when she'd accepted his proposal, when she'd agreed with all of his logical points. It had made *sense*.

Yet, looking at that bed piled high with pillows and flickering with candlelit shadows, there was nothing sensible about it.

'I almost forgot,' Paola said. 'Your husband left

this for you.' She gestured to a plain white box, wrapped with a ribbon of ivory silk.

'Oh?' Ana reached for it; the ribbon fell away with a slither and she opened the box. Inside was the most exquisite nightdress she'd ever seen; the silk was whisper-thin and delicately scalloped lace embroidered the edges. It was held up by two gauzy ribbons, to be tied at each shoulder.

'It's gorgeous,' Paola breathed, and Ana could only nod. Then she caught sight of the tag, and her heart sank straight down to her feet.

'It's also three sizes too big.'

'Men are terrible with things like that—' Paola said quickly, too quickly.

Ana nodded, tossing the gorgeous gown back into its box. 'Of course. It doesn't matter.' Yet it did. She felt hurt, ridiculously near tears, horribly vulnerable, and suddenly she wanted—needed—to be alone. 'I'm fine, Paola. Vittorio will most likely arrive soon. You can leave me.'

'Ana—'

'I'm fine,' she said again, more firmly, and then she gave her friend a quick kiss on the cheek. 'Thank you for all you've done, and for coming to be my bridesmaid. I know how sudden it all was—'

'That doesn't matter.' Paola hugged her tightly for a moment before releasing her and stepping back. 'Are you sure you'll be all right? I can wait—'

'No, I'd like a few moments alone.' Ana smiled, straightening her spine, throwing her shoulders back. When she spoke, her voice came out firm. 'Don't worry about me, Paola. I'll be fine.' If she kept saying it, perhaps she would believe it.

When she was alone, Ana spared that gown one more accusing glance and then she moved around the room, pacing, anxiety taking the place of her earlier resolve. She told herself it hardly mattered that the gown was three sizes too big, yet no matter how many times she repeated the words, a desperate litany, she couldn't believe it.

She felt that it did matter. She felt that Vittorio must secretly think she was plain and overweight and he couldn't possibly desire her at all, unless fortified with a great deal of very good whisky. Each thought, each realization, was like a direct hit to her self-confidence, a dagger wound to her heart.

An hour passed in agonizing slowness. She wanted him to come; she didn't want him to come. She wanted to confront him; she wanted to hide. She was annoyed with herself and her own absurd indecision. For ten years she'd been in control of things—of the winery, of her life, of her own emotions. Admittedly, it hadn't been a very exciting life, but she'd been purposeful and determined and *happy*.

Now she felt completely lost, adrift in the bewildering sea of her emotions. It was a sensation she did not enjoy at all.

When a light knock sounded on the door, Ana was almost relieved. Anything at that point was better than waiting. She'd found a thick terry cloth dressing gown in the wardrobe and she'd thrown it on, belting it tightly around her waist so she was covered nearly from her neck to her ankles.

'Where have you been?' she demanded before she'd even laid eyes on him properly; too late, she realized she sounded rather shrewish.

'I thought you'd appreciate a bit of time alone,' Vittorio replied mildly.

Ana swallowed all the hurt and disappointment and nodded stiffly. 'Yes, well. Thank you.'

'Apparently I thought wrong?' he asked, moving past her into the bedroom.

'I just wondered where you were.'

Standing in the middle of the sumptuous bedroom, Vittorio looked utterly in his element. He'd removed his tie and jacket and the top two buttons of his crisp white shirt were undone. His hair was a little rumpled, and Ana could see the shadow of stubble on his strong jaw. He looked unbearably sexy and suddenly, despite everything, she felt faint with longing. She sagged against the door.

Vittorio held up a bottle he was carrying. 'I brought you a wedding present.'

'Oh?' Ana glanced at it. 'Whisky,' she said a bit flatly, and tried to smile. 'Thank you.'

'You did express a preference for it,' Vittorio replied in that same mild voice that Ana wasn't sure she liked. It was so damn unemotional, and here she was, feeling utterly fraught.

'Actually,' she told him, 'I lied.' She enjoyed the

look of surprise on his face, his jaw slackening for a second. 'I don't really like whisky. That is, I haven't tried it very much.'

'Really.'

'Really.' Ana strode across the room and plucked the bottle from Vittorio's hand. 'I only said that because I could see how intent you were on manufacturing some kind of businesslike atmosphere, and it seemed like a bottle of whisky would help that.'

'Or we could have just had coffee,' Vittorio replied with the flicker of a smile.

'Coffee over billiards?' Ana arched an eyebrow. 'I don't think so. Anyway, since you brought it, why don't we have a glass now?'

'I thought you said you didn't like it.'

'Oh, didn't I tell you?' Ana gave him a wicked little smile. 'I've developed a taste for it, after all.'

Vittorio paused; Ana could see he was trying to gauge her mood, to decide what was the best—the most efficient and effective—thing to do now. Well, she was tired of that kind of attitude. Just like the last time they'd drunk whisky together, she felt reckless and defiant and even a little dangerous; it was not a pleasant feeling but it made her feel *alive*. She raised the bottle. 'Are there any glasses around?'

'I'm sure I can find some,' Vittorio murmured and moved past her to the en suite bathroom. He returned with two water tumblers and handed them over. 'No ice, I'm afraid.'

'That's all right. I've found I prefer it straight.'

'As do I,' he murmured. He was standing close to her so his breath tickled her ear, making her want to shiver. She just barely suppressed the urge and unscrewed the bottle, pouring two rather large whiskies. She handed Vittorio one of the glasses.

'*Cento anni di salute e felicità*,' he said with a wry twist to his mouth; it was the traditional wedding toast. A hundred years of health and happiness.

Ana nodded jerkily, and they drank at the same time.

In the aftermath of the alcohol her eyes burned and watered. She just barely kept herself from choking.

'All right?' Vittorio asked, putting his glass aside, and Ana smiled defiantly.

'Never better.'

For a second, his expression flickered. 'Ana—'

'Thank you for the gown, by the way. It's gorgeous.'

'Gown?' Vittorio repeated a bit warily and Ana smiled, the curve of her mouth forced and over-bright.

'This.' She reached for the box with its rather large scrap of silk. 'Am I meant to wear it tonight? Because I'm afraid it's a bit too big.' She gave a little laugh. 'I'm not actually as large as you think I am, I suppose.'

Vittorio took the gown without speaking, shook it out and gazed at it with a rather clinical eye. 'I see. It is a beautiful gown, Ana, but I'm afraid I didn't give it to you. I've learned my lesson with you where clothes are concerned.'

Now Ana's jaw slackened, the wind leaking right out of her self-righteous sails. 'You didn't send it?'

'No. But I can guess who did.'

'Who?'

'My mother. To send you a gown several sizes too big—this is the kind of thing she would do. Her little attempt to wound. It stings, *si*?' His eyes hardened. 'Trust me, I know.'

Suddenly the gown didn't matter at all. 'Vittorio—what has happened between you and your mother? And your brother too? Why are you all so—so terrible to one another? So cold.'

Vittorio was silent for a moment, before he shook his head. 'It is past, Ana, past and forgotten. There is nothing you need to know.'

'But it isn't really forgotten, is it? I can tell by the way you talk about it, even now—'

'It's late—' he cut her off '—and you need your sleep. I'll see you in the morning.'

Disappointment opened up inside her, a vast looming pit. She wanted to ask him to stay, but she knew she wouldn't. Couldn't begin their marriage this way, with her begging for him, for his touch. Yet why was he leaving? Was this his so-called sensitivity or merely his indifference? 'All right,' she whispered, her voice catching on the words.

He reached out with one hand and touched her cheek, his thumb finding that secret place where a tear had once sparkled. Ana closed her eyes and nearly swayed where she stood. 'It will be all right, *rondinella*,' he murmured. 'I know this is hard now—awkward too, for both of us, but it will be all right.'

Ana swallowed and nodded, her throat too tight to speak. She didn't open her eyes for a moment and, when she did, Vittorio had already gone.

Alone in the hallway, Vittorio cursed under his breath. Of course his mother would seek to discredit him with Ana from the first moment of their marriage. Of course she would find ways to weaken the tenuous link he'd forged with his bride. And, if Constantia stayed here, she would continue to poison Ana's mind and pare away her self-confidence.

Yet he knew he would not ask his mother to leave. He'd never asked her to leave. He'd been the one to leave, all those years ago; he'd felt like an interloper in his own home, unwanted and undesired, and it had been easier simply to walk away.

Vittorio thought of the disappointment he'd seen in Ana's eyes. She'd wanted him to stay; she'd even wanted him to make love to her. And he'd wanted it, too; his body even now stirred to lust. Yet he'd balked, like a shy virgin! The thought almost made him laugh in exasperation at his own reticence. All too easily he could imagine taking her in his arms, unwrapping her from that thick, bulky robe like a parcel from its paper.

Yet she wasn't merely a parcel, a thing, this wife

of his, and it was this uncomfortable new knowledge that kept him from staying. From consummating their marriage, for surely that was all it would be. A consummation, a soulless act, and he was—suddenly, stupidly too—afraid of hurting her.

Vittorio cursed aloud. Now was not the time to develop some kind of stupid sensitivity. He stopped, almost turned around, even if just to prove a point to himself. Then he remembered the way Ana's grey eyes, so wide and luminous and somehow soft, had darkened with disappointment when he'd said he was leaving, how her breath had shortened when he'd touched her cheek and, furious with himself, at a loss for what he should do now, he kept on walking.

CHAPTER EIGHT

THE next few days were some of the most depressing Ana had ever known, simply by reason of their utter sameness. Except for the fact that she drove back to Castle Cazlevara every night after work, Ana would not know she was married. Her days had not changed at all; after an impersonal breakfast with Vittorio, she left for the winery offices, spent the day there and returned to the castle for another impersonal and often silent meal.

Vittorio seemed to have retreated into himself; they hardly talked, and the little gifts he'd showered her with before their marriage had stopped completely. Ana couldn't tell if Vittorio was simply satisfied now he'd married her, or if he actually regretted the deed. As far as periods of adjustment went, theirs was an utter failure. There was no adjusting; there was only enduring.

Ana saw Constantia and Bernardo on occasion; they were currently residing at the castle, although they seemed to avoid both her and Vittorio. Bernardo ate out, and Constantia took her meals in her rooms.

It was, Ana reflected, an unhappy household, shrouded in its own misery.

After three days of this, Ana could take it no longer. She found Vittorio at the breakfast table, reading the newspaper and drinking his espresso. He barely glanced up when she entered.

'You'd think,' Ana said, hearing the acid in her own voice, 'that we'd been married three decades rather than three days.'

She saw Vittorio's fingers tense and then he lowered the newspaper. 'What do you mean, Ana?' he asked in that careful, mild voice he seemed to save just for her. It was so neutral, so *irritating*, for it made Ana feel as if he was dealing with a child or a puppy that needed training.

'I mean,' she retorted, as Giulia, the morning maid, came bustling forth with her own latte, 'that for the last three days—the only three days we've been married—you have been ignoring me. Are you regretting your decision, Vittorio? Because of course you know we can still get the marriage annulled.'

The only change in Vittorio's expression was a tightening of his lips and a flaring of his nostrils. 'I have no wish to annul this marriage.'

'You have no wish to act as if you were married, either.'

Vittorio folded his paper and dropped it on the table. He picked up his tiny cup of espresso and took a sip, studying Ana from over its rim. 'I wanted to

give you time,' he finally said quietly. 'I thought…
to rush into things might be difficult.'

'To feel like I don't belong—that we're not even
married—is difficult too,' Ana countered. His words
had comforted her, given her hope, but she wasn't
about to give up any ground quite yet.

Vittorio nodded slowly. 'Very well. I was drawing
up the guest list for the party I mentioned earlier.
I thought we could have it on Friday, in two days'
time. If you have anyone you'd like to add to the list,
just tell me, or email me the particulars.' He paused
before adding only a bit acerbically, 'Perhaps when
we announce to the world we are married, you will
feel it yourself.'

Or, Ana thought a bit savagely as Vittorio rose
and took his leave, perhaps she would feel married
when Vittorio treated her like a wife, a proper wife,
a wife in every sense of the word as he'd told her he
would.

Alone in the dining room, she drummed her fingers on the burnished mahogany table top and moodily sipped her latte. All around her the castle was
quiet; even though Giulia was undoubtedly hovering
just outside the door, Ana could hear nothing. She
felt very alone.

I didn't think it would be like this.

Annoyed with herself, Ana pushed the traitorous
thought aside and rose from the table. The dining
room, like many other rooms in the castle, had been
refurbished some time in the last century and now

possessed long elegant windows overlooking the terraced gardens that led down to the drained moat. Under a fragile blue sky, it was austerely beautiful, yet it hardly felt like home. And she still couldn't see or hear another living soul.

Without even realizing she was doing it, Ana brushed at the corner of her eye and her fingertip came away damp. She was crying. She never cried, not since her mother had died. Even during those miserable years at boarding school, that first seeming rejection of her father and, later, Roberto's worse rejection, she'd always choked her sorrow down and soldiered on so it remained a hot lump in her chest, pushing it further and further down until she couldn't feel it at all. Almost.

Now she felt it deeply, all the sorrow and anger and fear, rising up in a red tide of emotion she didn't have the time or energy to deal with.

She'd accepted that Vittorio didn't love her. She'd been prepared that he might not desire her the way she desired him. She hadn't counted on the fact that he'd actually avoid her.

How was this meant to make her life easier?

'Has Vittorio left you alone?'

Ana whirled around at the sound of her mother-in-law's clipped voice. The ageing beauty stood framed in the doorway of the dining room, poised as ever to make an entrance. Ana forced a small smile. She really didn't feel like dealing with Constantia just now.

'He went to work, and I'm off in a moment too,' she said, trying to sound cheerful even as she attempted some kind of regretful look that she wouldn't be able to spend breakfast with her mother-in-law. 'We're both very busy.'

'Of course you are.' Constantia glided into the room, followed by Giulia, who brought a separate tray of espresso and rolls. The Dowager Countess clearly deserved special service. 'Tell me, Anamaria,' Constantia asked as she sat down and neatly broke a roll in half, 'how is marriage suiting you?' She glanced up, her eyes narrowed only slightly, so Ana couldn't tell if her mother-in-law knew just what kind of marriage she and Vittorio had, or if she genuinely wanted to know the answer to that thorny question. Constantia never gave anything away.

Ana's mouth widened into a bright false smile. 'Wonderfully.'

Constantia nodded thoughtfully and nibbled a piece of her roll. 'Vittorio is so much like his father. A hard man to be married to.'

In a flash Ana remembered her own father's assessment of Arturo Cazlevara: *Arturo was a good man too, but he was hard. Without mercy.*

She glanced at Constantia, now composedly sipping her espresso, with genuine curiosity. 'What do you mean?'

Constantia shrugged one shoulder. 'Surely you know what I mean? Vittorio isn't…affectionate. Emotional.'

She paused, and when she spoke her voice sounded almost ragged. 'He will never love you.'

Something sharp lanced through Ana; she didn't know whether it was fear or pain. Perhaps both. She turned back to the window. 'I don't expect him to love me,' she said quietly.

'You may have convinced yourself of that once, my dear,' Constantia said. 'But can you continue to do so? For years?'

There was too much knowledge, too much sorrowful experience in the older woman's voice for Ana not to ask. 'Is that what happened to you?' Ana turned around; for a moment Constantia looked vulnerable, and her fingers shook a little bit as she replaced her cup in its saucer.

'Yes, it is. I loved Arturo Cazlevara from the time I was a little girl. We were neighbours, you know, just like Vittorio and you are—were. Everyone approved of the marriage, everyone thought it was a great match. Arturo never said he didn't love me, of course. And on the surface he was considerate, kind. Just like Vittorio, *si*? Yet here—' Constantia lightly touched her breastbone '—here, I knew.'

Tua cuore. Sudden tears stung Ana's eyes and she blinked them away. She was *not* going to cry. 'Consideration and kindness,' she said after a moment, 'count for much.'

Constantia laughed once, the sound sharp with cynicism. 'Oh, you think so? Because I happen to believe those agreeable sentiments make you feel like a puppy that has been patted on the head and told to go and lie down and stop bothering anyone anymore. Not a nice feeling all these years, you know? To feel like a dog.' She paused, and something hardened in both her face and voice. 'You would be amazed to know the things you can be driven to, the things you do even though you hate them—hate yourself—when you feel like that.' She drained her espresso and rose from the table, giving Ana one last cool smile. The haughty set of her shoulders and the arrogant tilt of her chin made Ana think Constantia regretted her moment of honesty. 'Perhaps it is different for you, Ana.'

'It *is* different,' Ana replied with sudden force. 'I don't love Vittorio either.'

Constantia's smile was pitying. 'Don't you?' she said, and walked from the room.

Constantia's words echoed through Ana's mind all morning as she tried to focus on work. She couldn't. She argued endlessly with herself, trying to convince herself that she didn't love Vittorio, she didn't love the way his eyes gleamed when he was amused, the way they softened when he spoke quietly, the broad set of his shoulders, the feel of his lips—

Of course, those were all physical attributes. You couldn't love someone based on how they *looked*. Yet Ana knew there was more to Vittorio than his dark good looks. When she was in his presence, she felt alive. Amazed. As if anything could happen, good or bad, and the good would be wonderful and even the bad would be all right because she still would be with him. She wanted to know more about him, not just to feel his body against hers, but his heart against hers also. She wanted to see him smile, just for her. To have him whisper something just meant for her.

She wanted him to love her. She wanted to love him.

She wanted love.

'No!' The word burst out of her, bounced around the walls of her empty room. 'No,' she said again, a whisper, a plea. She couldn't want love. She couldn't, because Vittorio would never give it. She thought of Constantia, her face a map of the disappointments life had given her. Ana didn't know all the history between Constantia and Vittorio, or Constantia and her own husband, but she knew—it was plain to see—that the woman was bitter, angry, and perhaps even in despair. She didn't want that. Yet, if she wanted Vittorio's love—which she was still trying to convince herself she didn't—it seemed like only a matter of time until she was like Constantia, unfulfilled and unhappy, pacing the rooms of Castle Cazlevara and cursing other people's joy.

That afternoon Ana left work early—a rare occurrence—and drove to the Mestre train station that crossed the lagoon into Venice. As she rode over the Ponte della Libertà—the Bridge of Liberty—Ana wondered what she was doing…and why. Why had she summoned all her courage and rung the boutique

Vittorio had taken her to before their marriage, why had she made an appointment with the pencil-thin Feliciana to be fitted for several outfits, including a gown for the party on Friday night?

Ana told herself it was because she needed some new clothes, now that she was the Countess. Part of her arrangement with Vittorio was that she would dress appropriately to her station, as he'd said. Naturally, it made sense to visit the boutique he'd chosen above all others for this purpose.

Yet, no matter how many times Ana told herself this—mustering all her logic, her common sense— her heart told her otherwise. She was doing this— dressing this way—because she wanted Vittorio to see her differently. She wanted him to see her as a wife, and not just any wife, but a wife he could love.

The thought terrified her.

'Contessa Cazlevara!' Feliciana started forward the minute Ana entered the narrow confines of the upscale boutique. Ana smiled and allowed herself to be air-kissed, even though she felt awkward and cloddish and, well, *huge* in this place. Feliciana had to be a good eight inches shorter than her, at the very least.

'I've put some things aside for you,' Feliciana said, leading her to a private salon in the back of the boutique, 'that I think will suit you very well.'

'Really?' Ana couldn't keep the scepticism from her voice. Feliciana had only glimpsed her once before; how on earth could she know what suited her? And a little mocking voice asked, how could *anything* suit her?

Ana commanded that voice to be silent. Yet other voices rose to take its place: the locker room taunts of the girls at boarding school, the boys who had ignored or teased her, the helpless sigh of the matron who had shaken her head and said, 'At least you're strong.' And then, most damning of all, Roberto's utter rejection. *How could I?*

Over the years she'd avoided places like this, dresses like these, for a reason. And now, standing in the centre of a brightly lit, mirrored dressing room while Feliciana bustled over with an armful of frocks, she felt horribly exposed and vulnerable.

'Now, first I thought, a gown for the party, *si*?' Feliciana smiled. 'Most important.'

'Yes, I suppose,' Ana murmured, looking dubiously at a white lace gown she'd glimpsed on her last visit to the boutique. It now hung over Feliciana's arm, exquisite and fragile.

'A formal occasion, is it not? I thought we'd try this.' Feliciana held up the gown.

Ana shook her head. 'I don't think…'

'You'll see,' Feliciana said firmly. She gestured to Ana's trouser suit with a tiny grimace of distaste. 'Now, you hide yourself in these clothes, as if you are ashamed.'

Ana flushed. 'I'm just not—'

'But you *are*,' Feliciana interjected. She smiled,

laying a hand on Ana's arm. 'It is not my job to make women look awkward or ugly, *si*? I know what I am doing. Right now, you walk with your shoulders stooped, your head bowed as if you are trying not to be tall.'

'I don't—' Ana protested.

'You are tall,' Feliciana said firmly. 'With a beautiful full figure. And don't you know many women long to be so tall? You are strikingly beautiful, but I know you don't think you are.' She let go of Ana's shoulders and gestured to the lace confection of a dress. 'In this, you will see.' She smiled again, softly. 'Trust me.'

So Ana did. She took the dress and let Feliciana take her trouser suit, slipping into the lacy sheath with some foreboding and also a building excitement. The dress fitted like a second skin, hugging her hips, the dip of her waist and the swell of her breasts. Its plunging neckline was made respectable by the handmade Burano lace edging it, and the material ended in a frothy swirl around her ankles. Ana sucked her stomach in as Feliciana did up the hidden zipper in the back, but there was no need as the dress fitted perfectly. They *did* make gowns like this in her size.

Ana didn't dare look in the mirror. She wasn't afraid, precisely, but neither did she want to be disappointed.

'*Uno minuto...*' Feliciana muttered, surveying her, her hands on her hips. She reached out and tugged the clip from Ana's hair; it cascaded down her back in a dark swirl. 'Ah...*perfectto*!'

Perfect? Her? Ana almost shook her head, but Feliciana steered her towards the mirror. 'Look. You've never seen yourself in something like this before, have you?'

No, she hadn't. Ana knew that the minute she gazed at her reflection, because for a second at least she couldn't believe she was staring at herself. She was staring at a stranger, a woman—a gorgeous, confident, sexy woman. She shook her head.

'No...'

Feliciana clucked in dismay. 'You don't like it?'

'No.' A bubble of laughter erupted, escaping through her lips as Ana turned around. 'I don't like it. I love it.'

Feliciana grinned. '*Buon*. Because I have at least six other gowns I want you to try.'

By the time Ana left the boutique, she'd purchased four gowns, several skirts and tops, three pairs of shoes, including a pair of silver stilettos that she'd balked at until Feliciana had told her sternly, 'Your husband must be almost five inches taller than you. You can wear heels.'

She'd never worn heels in her life. She'd probably fall on her face. Ana giggled; she wasn't used to making such a girlish sound. Yet right now she felt girlish, feminine and frivolous and *fun*. She'd enjoyed this afternoon and, best of all, she couldn't *wait* until Vittorio saw her in the lace gown on Friday night.

Yet, when Friday night actually came and she stood at the top of the sweeping staircase that led down to the castle's foyer and its waiting master, Ana didn't feel so confident. So *fun*. She felt sick with nerves, with a queasy fear that Vittorio wouldn't like how she looked or, worse, that he wouldn't even care how she looked. They'd barely seen each other outside meals and Ana spent her nights alone. She was a wife in name only, and she longed to change that tonight.

From the top of the stairs she could see him waiting at the bottom, could feel his impatience. He wore a perfectly cut suit of grey silk and he rested one long tapered hand on the banister railing.

'Ana?' he called up, a bit sharply. 'Are you ready? The guests will be here very soon.'

'Yes,' she called, her own voice wavering a little. 'I'm ready.'

Vittorio heard Ana coming down the stairs behind him, but he didn't turn around right away. He needed to steel himself, he realized, for however his wife might look. So far he had not been impressed with her clothes; her wedding dress had been an unmitigated disaster. She'd told him she knew the difference between a designer gown and a bin bag, but Vittorio had yet to be convinced. Not, he reflected, that he'd taken Ana's dress sense into consideration when he'd chosen her as his bride.

Why *had* he chosen her as his bride? Vittorio wondered rather moodily. All the businesslike reasons about merging wineries and knowing the region seemed utterly absurd to base a marriage on. Of course, when his mother had spoken to him about heirs, his logical mind had not thought about a *marriage*; it had simply fastened on the one necessity: wife. Object. Then he'd seen the vulnerability in Ana's eyes, had felt her softness against him, had breathed in the earthy scent of her desire and known that *wife* and *object* were not two words ever to string together.

Ana was a person, and not just a person, but his *wife*. His beloved. The person he should protect and cherish above all others. The person, he realized bleakly, he was meant to love. And he had no idea what to do with her.

It was why he'd avoided her since their wedding; why he still had not come to her bed. He'd thought he could live with a business arrangement. That was what he had wanted. Yet now, bizarrely, he found the cold-blooded terms of their arrangement to be... distasteful. Yet he didn't love Ana, didn't know if he was even capable of such an emotion. He hadn't loved anyone in years. His entire adult life had been focused on *not* loving, on building Cazlevara Wines, maintaining his reputation and influence as Count, trying to forget the fractured family he'd left behind.

The women he'd involved himself with hadn't even come close to touching his heart.

Yet *Ana*…Ana with her blunt way of speaking and her soft grey eyes, her brash confidence and her lurking vulnerability, her tall, lush figure and her earthy scent…Ana somehow slipped inside the defences he'd erected around himself, his heart. He'd prided himself on being logical, sensible, perhaps even cold. Yet now he wouldn't even go to his wife's bed for fear of—what? Hurting her?

He'd told his bride very plainly that he never intended to love her. Love, he had said, was a destructive emotion. And perhaps that was what made him afraid now; he was afraid that his love would destroy Ana, would ruin their marriage.

His love was destructive.

'Vittorio…?' He felt Ana's hand on his sleeve, her voice no more than an uncertain whisper. She must have been standing there for some moments, waiting for him to notice her while he was lost in his gloomy reflections. Vittorio turned around.

'Good even—' He stopped, the words dried in his mouth, his head suddenly, completely empty of thoughts. The woman in front of him was stunning, a vision of ethereal loveliness in white lace. No, he realized distantly, she wasn't ethereal. She was earthy and real and so very beautiful. And she was his wife. 'You look…' he began and, though she tried to disguise it, he saw Ana's face fall, the disappointment shadowing her eyes and making her shoulders slump just a fraction. He let himself touch her, holding her by the shoulders. Her skin was warm and golden. The dress clung to her figure; he'd never realized how perfectly she was proportioned, the swell of her breasts and the curve of her hips. He'd once considered her mannish; the thought was now laughable. He'd never seen a more feminine woman. 'You look amazing,' he said, his voice low, heartfelt, and Ana smiled.

She had the most amazing smile. He'd noticed her teeth before, straight and white, as one might notice a piece of workmanship. Now he saw the way the smile transformed her face, softened the angles and made joy dance in her eyes in golden glints.

Amazing. His wife was amazing.

'Thank you,' she said, her voice just as heartfelt, and Vittorio did the only thing he could do… He kissed her. As he drew her close, he was conscious of her generous curves fitting so snugly against his own body, amazed at the way her length lined up to his. How had he ever stooped to kiss a shorter woman before? His back ached just to think of it.

And Ana's lips… They were soft and warm and as generous as the rest of her, open and giving and so very sweet. Vittorio had meant only to kiss her briefly—something between a peck and a brush—but once he tasted her he found he couldn't get enough. The kiss went on and on, her arms snaking up around his shoulders, her body pressing against his—she'd never been shy—until someone behind him cleared his throat in a pointed manner.

'Pardon me for breaking up this rather touching scene,' Bernardo drawled, 'but the guests are starting to arrive.'

'Good.' Vittorio stepped away from Ana, his arm still around her waist. She *fitted* against him, nestled near him in a way that was neither cloying nor coy. It was, he knew, as genuine as the rest of her was.

Bernardo eyed Ana with obvious surprise. 'You cleaned up rather well.'

'Bernardo,' Vittorio said sharply, 'that is no way to speak to my wife the Countess.'

Bernardo turned back to Vittorio, his eyebrows raised. 'Isn't it what you were thinking?' he countered. Vittorio pressed his lips together; he didn't want to argue with his brother now. He wouldn't spoil this evening for Ana. Bernardo turned to Ana and made a little bow. 'Forgive me, Ana. I meant no insult. You look very beautiful.'

Vittorio said nothing. This was how his brother always acted; he'd deliver the sting with one hand and the sweetness with the other. It made it impossible to fight him, or at least to win. Vittorio had learned this long ago, when his parents had drawn the battle lines. Constantia got Bernardo and his father took him. They had been his parents' most potent weapons. It had, Vittorio reflected, been a long drawn-out war.

'No offence taken, Bernardo,' Ana said, smiling. 'I was thinking the same thing myself.'

Bernardo gave her an answering flicker of a smile and bowed again. Vittorio squeezed Ana's waist and the first guests came towards them before he could thank his wife for being so gracious.

Ana moved through the party in a haze of happiness. She never wanted to forget the look on Vittorio's face when he'd turned around and seen her. She'd expected the disbelief, of course, but not the joy. He'd been *happy* to see her. He'd wanted her by his side. And when he'd kissed her… Every secret hope and latent need had risen up inside her on newly formed wings, and she hadn't suppressed them or forced them back to the ground. For years she'd refused to entertain such dreams, knowing they could only lead to disappointment, yet when Vittorio had looked at her, she'd felt like the woman she'd always longed to be. The woman she was meant to be. It was a wonderful feeling.

She stayed by Vittorio's side for most of the party. He wanted her there, kept his arm around her, her hip pressed against his. She laughed and chatted and listened and nodded, but none of it really penetrated. The need—the desire—was building within her slowly, a force rising up and needing to be reckoned with. To be satisfied.

Tonight, she told herself. *Tonight, he will come*

to me. As the evening wore on, her certainty—and her happiness—only grew.

Vittorio had been so proud, so happy to have Ana by his side. He'd drifted through the party in a haze, on a cloud. He couldn't wait to get Ana alone, to touch her—

Yet now she'd gone to see her father off and, alone, he felt strangely flat, indifferent to all he'd achieved. He wanted her to come back to him and yet, even so, he didn't go in search of her. He didn't even know what he would say.

He thought of how Enrico Viale had stopped him in the middle of the party, one hand on his sleeve. 'She looked beautiful, our Ana, *si*?' the older man had said, pride shining in his eyes. Vittorio had been about to agree when he realized Enrico was not talking about how Ana looked tonight. 'It was her mother's wedding dress, you know. I asked her to wear it.'

Vittorio had been left speechless, amazed and humbled by Ana's selflessness, by her loyalty. And he'd demanded that same loyalty of her for *him*? When he didn't even know what to do with her, how to treat her, how to *love* her?

Love. But he didn't *want* love.

As the last guests trickled outside, the cars heading down the castle's steep drive in a steady stream of light, Vittorio wondered what on earth he'd been trying to accomplish by setting out to acquire a wife like so much baggage. What had been the point, to take another being into his care, another life into his hands? Who was meant to notice, to know?

Who cared?

Of course, most of his neighbours and fellow wine-makers were curious about the Count of Cazlevara's sudden return and even more sudden marriage. He'd felt their implicit approval that he'd returned to where he belonged, was now taking his rightful place, es-teemed winemaker and leader of the community.

Yet he hadn't been trying to gain *their* approval. At that moment, their approval hardly mattered at all.

'So, Vittorio. A success.'

Vittorio turned slowly around; his mother stood in the doorway of the drawing room. She looked coldly elegant in a cream satin sheath dress, her expres-sion unsmiling. This was the person whose approval he'd been trying to gain, Vittorio realized, and how absurd that was, considering his mother had not had a moment of interest or affection for him since he was four. When his brother had been born.

He was jealous, Vittorio realized, incredulous and yet still somehow unsurprised by this. All these years, his desire to return to his home and show his brother and mother his success, his self-suffi-ciency—it had just been jealousy. Petty, pathetic jealousy.

He turned back to the window. The last cars

had disappeared down the darkened drive. 'So it appears.'

'You're not pleased?' she asked, moving into the room. He heard a caustic note in her voice that still made his shoulders tense and the vulnerable space between them prickle.

Go away, Vittorio. Leave me alone.

At that moment he felt like that confused child who had tugged his mother's sleeve, desperate to show her a drawing, receive a hug. She'd turned away, time and time again, forever averting both her face and her heart. When she'd welcomed Bernardo, adored and doted on and spoiled him utterly, it seemed obvious. She simply preferred his brother to him.

Vittorio made an impatient sound of disgust; he was disgusted with himself. Why was he remembering these silly, childish moments now? He'd lived with his mother's rejection for most of his life. He'd learned not to care. He'd steeled himself against it, against the treachery she'd committed when his father had died—

Except obviously he hadn't, for the emotions were still present, raked up and raw, and they made him angry. What kind of man was still hurt by his *mother*? It was ridiculous, pathetic, shaming.

'On the contrary, Mother. I am very pleased.' His voice was bland with just a hint of sharpness; it was the tone he always reserved for her.

She gave an answering little laugh, just as sharp. 'Oh, Vittorio. Nothing is ever enough, is it? You're just like your father.' The words were meant to be an accusation, a condemnation.

'I'll take that as a compliment.'

His mother's lip curled in a sneer. 'Of course you will.'

Impatient with all her veiled little barbs, Vittorio shrugged. 'Where's Ana?'

Constantia arched her eyebrows in challenge. 'Why do you care?'

His temper finally frayed. 'Because she is my *wife*.' And he wanted to know where she was, he wanted to see her now, to feel her smile, her sweetness—

'A wife you won't love.'

Vittorio stiffened. 'That is no concern of—'

'Isn't it?' She stepped closer and he saw the anger in her eyes, as well as something else. Something that looked strangely like sorrow. It was unfamiliar. He was used to his mother angry, but sad—?

'You don't know what it is like to love someone, Vittorio, who will never love you back—'

He laughed in disbelief; he couldn't help it. 'Don't I?'

Constantia looked utterly nonplussed. 'No—'

He shook his head, too weary to explain. 'Do you know where Ana is?'

'You will bring heartache to that girl. You will destroy her—'

Vittorio tensed, steeling himself once more, but this time he couldn't. *Love is a destructive emotion.*

The thought of bringing such pain and misery to Ana made his head bow, his shoulders shake. 'Why do you care?' he asked in a low, savage voice.

'She is a good woman, Vittorio.'

'Too good for me, obviously.'

Constantia sighed impatiently. 'I have made many mistakes with you, I know. I have many regrets. But this marriage—it can only lead to more despair. And surely our family has had enough unhappiness?'

She was pleading with him, as if their family's misery was his fault? Vittorio turned around, his body rigid with rage. 'On that point we agree, Mother. Yet it seems odd that the instrument of so much unhappiness should then seek to end it.'

Constantia blinked as if she'd been struck. 'I know you blame me—'

'Blame you?' Vittorio repeated silkily. 'Are you referring to your attempt to take my inheritance, my father only *hours* in the grave? Your desperate desire to drag the family into the law courts and give my brother my title?'

Constantia straightened and met his hostile gaze directly. 'Yes, Vittorio, I am referring to that. God knows you will never let me forget it.'

'One hardly forgets the dagger thrust between one's shoulders,' Vittorio returned, every word encased in ice. He still remembered how he had reeled with shock; he'd come back from his father's funeral, devastated by grief, only to find that in his absence his mother had met a solicitor and attempted

to overturn the contents of his father's will, disin-
heriting him completely and giving everything to
Bernardo. All the childhood slights had led to that
one brutal moment, when he'd understood with stark
clarity that his mother didn't just dislike him, she
despised him. She'd do anything to keep him from
inheriting what was rightfully his.

He would never forget. He couldn't.

'No,' Constantia agreed softly, her eyes glittering,
'one does not forget. And I will tell you, Vittorio,
that for a woman to be denied love—by her own
husband—is not a dagger between the shoulders,
but one straight to the heart. For your wife's sake, if
not my own, do not hurt her.'

'Such pretty words,' Vittorio scoffed. The rage
had left him, making him feel only weary. 'You have
come to care for my wife then, Mother?'

'I know how she feels,' Constantia said bleakly
and, with one last shake of her head, she left the
room.

Her words rang in his ears, and yet Vittorio still
made himself dismiss them. *I know how she feels.*
Was his mother implying she'd loved his father? To
Vittorio's young eyes, his parents had agreed on a
polite marriage of convenience. Just like the one
he'd meant to have. Yet his parents' marriage had
descended into anger and even hatred, and at the
thought of that happening to him—to Ana—Vittorio
swore aloud. All the old feelings, hurt memories, had
been raked up tonight and Vittorio knew why.

Ana.

Somehow she'd affected him, touched him in a way he had never been touched. Made him open and exposed and, more than that, she made him want. Made him need.

Love.

He swore again.

'Vittorio?'

He whirled around. Ana stood in the doorway, her face nearly as white as her lace gown.

'How much did you hear?' he asked, his tone brusque, brutal.

Ana flinched. 'Enough. Too much.'

'I told you my family's history was not worth repeating,' Vittorio replied with a shrug. He moved to the drinks table and poured himself a whisky.

'Don't—' Ana said inadvertently and he turned around, one eyebrow arched.

'I'm having a *drink*, Ana,' he said, the words a taunt. 'Whisky. Your favourite. Don't you want to join me?'

'No. Vittorio, I want to talk.'

He took a healthy swallow and let the alcohol burn straight to his gut. 'Go ahead.'

Ana flinched again. Vittorio knew he was being callous, even cruel, but he couldn't help it. The exchange with his mother, the emerging feelings for Ana—it all left him feeling so exposed. Vulnerable.

Afraid.

He hated it.

Turning away from her, he kept his voice a bored drawl. 'So what do you want to talk about?'

Ana watched her husband as he gazed out of the window, affecting an air of bored indifference, yet she knew better now. He was hurting. She didn't understand everything he'd referred to in his conversation with Constantia, didn't know the source of all the pain, but she did know her marriage had no chance if Vittorio was going to remain mired in his painful past.

'Tell me what went wrong,' she said quietly.

Vittorio must not have been expecting that, for he bowed his head suddenly, his fingers clenched around his whisky glass.

'Everything,' he finally said in a low voice. 'Everything went wrong.'

Cautiously Ana approached him, laid a hand on his shoulder. 'Oh, Vittorio—'

He jerked away. 'Don't pity me. I could not stand that.'

'I just want to understand—'

'It's simple, Ana.' He turned to face her, his expression hard and implacable once more. 'My mother didn't love me. What a sad story, eh? Pathetic, no? A thirty-seven-year-old man whingeing on about his mean *mamma*.'

'There's more to it than that,' Ana said quietly.

'Oh, a few trite details.' He gave a negligent

shrug and drained his glass. 'You see, my parents hated each other. Perhaps there was once love or at least affection, but not so I could remember. By the time Bernardo came along, the battle lines were drawn. I belonged to my father and Bernardo was my mother's.'

'What do you mean?'

'Simple. My father had no time or patience for Bernardo, and my mother had none for me. They used us like weapons. And my father was a good man, he trained me well—'

'But he was a hard man,' Ana interjected, remembering.

Vittorio glanced at her sharply. 'Who told you that?'

'My father. He said Arturo was a good man, but without mercy.'

Vittorio let out a little breath of sound; Ana wasn't sure if it was a laugh or something else. Perhaps even a sob. 'Perhaps that is true. But he knew I was to inherit, and he wanted to train me up for the role—'

Ana could just imagine what that must have felt like, especially if Bernardo was not receiving the same harsh treatment. 'And Bernardo?' she asked softly.

'My mother lavished all her love on him. He was like a spoilt poodle.'

Ana flinched at the contempt in his voice. Surely being spoiled was just as bad as being disciplined, just in a different way. 'It sounds like both of you had difficult childhoods.'

'Both of us?' Vittorio repeated in disbelief, then shrugged. 'Maybe.' He sounded bored, and Ana clung to her belief that it was merely a cover for the true, deeper emotions he was too afraid to expose.

She knew all about being vulnerable. Physically and emotionally. Even wearing this dress—opening herself to scorn—made her feel exposed, as exposed as Vittorio did raking through his unhappy childhood. No one liked to talk about such dark memories, admit how they hurt.

'What happened when your father died?' Ana asked.

'My mother did what she'd undoubtedly been planning to do ever since Bernardo was born. She went to court to have his will overturned—and Bernardo made heir.'

Ana gasped. Even though she'd suspected as much, it still surprised her. Why would Constantia do such a vindictive thing? Yet, even as she asked the question, Ana thought she knew the answer. Hadn't Constantia explained it herself? *You would be amazed to know the things you can be driven to... when you feel like that.* And then, her words tonight: *You're just like your father.* Had she transferred all the bitterness and anger she'd felt towards her husband to her son? It seemed perfectly possible, and unbearably sad.

'Oh, Vittorio,' Ana whispered. 'I am sorry.'

'Well, don't be,' he replied, his voice turning harsh again. 'She didn't have a prayer of succeeding. My father was too smart for that. Perhaps he suspected what she was up to, what she could be capable of. His will remained intact, and Bernardo didn't inherit a single *lira*.'

Ana gasped again. 'Not…anything?'

'No, and rightly so. He would have squandered it all.'

'But then,' Ana said slowly, realization dawning, 'he lives here only on your sufferance. Doesn't he work at the winery?'

Vittorio shrugged. 'I let him work as the assistant manager.'

'You let him,' Ana repeated. 'As an assistant.'

'Are you saying it is not enough?' Vittorio demanded raggedly. 'This brother who would have taken everything from me? Do you think he would have been so merciful?'

Ana shook her head. 'But if your mother attempted all this with the will when your father died, you were only—'

'Fourteen.'

'And Bernardo was a child—nine or ten at the most—'

'Ten,' Vittorio confirmed flatly. Anger sparked in his eyes; his face had become hard again, a stranger's. 'Are you taking his side, Ana? Don't you remember what I told you, what I warned you about?'

His tone was so dangerous, so icy, that Ana could

only blink in confusion, her mind whirling with all these revelations. 'What—?'

Vittorio closed the space between them, circling her wrist with his hands, drawing her to him. The movement was not one of seduction, but possession, and Ana came up hard against his chest. 'Loyalty, Ana. I told you those closest to me would try to discredit me. You swore you would be loyal to me—'

She could hardly believe he was bringing up loyalty now. This was his *family*. 'Vittorio, I am simply trying to understand—'

'Maybe I don't want you to understand,' Vittorio said harshly. 'Maybe if you understood—' He stopped, shaking his head, a look of what almost seemed like fear flashing across his face before he muttered an oath and then, with a sudden groan, claimed her mouth in a kiss.

It wasn't a kiss, Ana thought distantly, so much as a brand. He was punishing her for her curiosity and reminding her of her vow. And, in that kiss she felt all his anger, his hurt and even his fear. And despite her own answering anger—that he would kiss her this way—she felt the traitorous flicker of her own desire and she pressed against him, let her hands tangle in his hair, wanting to change this angry embrace into something healing and *good*—

'No!' With a bellow of disgust, Vittorio pushed her away. Ana stumbled and reached out to steady herself; both of them were gasping as if they'd run a race. And lost.

'Vittorio—'

'No,' he said again. He raked a hand through his hair, let out a ragged sob. 'Not like this. God help me, I never wanted this.'

'But—'

'I told you,' he said in a low voice, 'love is a destructive emotion.'

Ana shook her head, wanting to deny what he said, wanting to fight—and wondering if he was actually telling her, in a terribly twisted way, that he loved her.

Was this love? This confusion and sorrow and pain?

No wonder they'd both agreed to live without it.

'It doesn't have to be destructive,' Ana said quietly but, his back now to her, Vittorio just shook his head.

'With me,' he said in a voice so low Ana strained to hear, 'it is.' He let out a shuddering sigh. 'Leave me, Ana. Just leave me.'

Ana stood there uncertainly, knowing to slink away now was surely the worst thing to do. 'No,' she said finally. 'I don't want to.'

Vittorio swung around, incredulous. 'What—'

'We're married, Vittorio. I'm not going to run away like some frightened child.' He flinched, and she raised her chin. 'And I'm not going to sleep alone tonight, either. I'm your wife and I belong in your bed.'

Vittorio's disbelief turned to disdain. *'Now—'*

She stepped closer to him, reached out with one hand to touch his lapel. 'Just hold me, Vittorio.' She saw his mouth tremble and she touched his lips. 'And let me hold you. And maybe, together, for a few moments, we can forget all this bitterness and pain.'

Vittorio shook his head slowly and Ana's heart sank. She'd thought she'd reached him, managed to get past the barrier he'd constructed to keep her—and anyone important—out. She could not bear his rejection now, not when she'd made herself so vulnerable, so exposed—just as he had—

Then, to her amazement and joy, he slowly reached for her hand, lacing his fingers tightly with hers, and silently, accepting, he led her from the darkened room.

CHAPTER NINE

ANA woke to sunlight. Even better, warming her deep inside, she woke with Vittorio's arm around her, her head nestled against his shoulder. She breathed in the scent of his skin, loving it, loving him.

Yes, she loved him. It seemed so obvious, so simple, in the clean, healing light of day. Yes, love was confusing and scary and full of sorrow and pain; it was *love*. Opening your heart and your body and even your soul to another person. Risking everything, your own health and happiness and well-being. And yet gaining so much.

Maybe.

She pulled away from Vittorio a little so she could look at him; he remained asleep, his features softened, almost gentle in repose. She touched the dark stubble on his chin, felt her heart twist painfully. Yes, love hurt.

This love hurt—for, if she loved him, she had no idea if he loved her.

Love is a destructive emotion.

She was starting to understand why he believed such a thing. Constantia's love for her husband had been destructive, her unhappiness and despair leading her to unhealthy relationships with both of her sons. And, as the one who felt unloved by his mother—and harshly loved, no doubt, by his father—Ana could almost understand why Vittorio wanted no more of it.

My love wouldn't be destructive. My love would heal you.

She touched his cheek, let her fingers feather over his eyebrow. He stirred and she stilled, holding her breath, not wanting him to wake up and ruin this moment. She was afraid when he opened his eyes the distance would be back, the cold, logical man who had insisted on a marriage of convenience, a marriage without love.

And she had agreed. She had, somehow, managed to convince herself that that was the kind of marriage, the kind of life, she wanted. Lying there, half in his arms, Ana knew it was not and never had been. She'd accepted such a poor bargain simply because she was afraid she'd find nothing else—and because it had been a bargain with Vittorio.

A life with Vittorio.

When had she started loving him? The seeds had surely been sown long ago, when he had touched her cheek and called her swallow. Such a small moment, yet in it she'd seen his gentleness, his tender heart, and she hoped—prayed—that she could see them again now. Soon.

She wouldn't let Vittorio push her away or keep their marriage as coldly convenient—and safe—as he wanted it to be.

Ana eased herself out of Vittorio's embrace, wondering just how she could accomplish such a herculean task. She'd agreed to a loveless marriage, very clearly. How could she now change the terms and expect Vittorio to agree?

Lying there in a pool of sunlight, still warmed by Vittorio's touch, the answer was obvious. By having him fall in love with her.

And Ana thought she knew just how to begin.

Vittorio awoke slowly, stretching languorously, feeling more relaxed and rested than he had in months. Years. He blinked at the sunlight streaming in through the windows and then shifted his weight, suddenly, surprisingly, *alarmingly* conscious of the empty space by him in the bed.

Ana was gone.

It shouldn't bother him—hurt him—for, God knew, he was used to sleeping alone. Even when he was involved with a woman, he left her bed—or made her leave his—well before dawn. It had been his standard practice, and he neither questioned it nor chose to change it.

Now, however, he realized how alone he felt. How lonely.

'Good morning, sleepy-head.'

Vittorio turned, his body relaxing once more at the sight of Ana in the doorway of his bedroom, wearing nothing but his shirt from last night. He could see the shadowy vee of her breasts disappearing between the buttons, the shirt tails just skimming her thighs. She looked wonderfully feminine, incredibly sexy. Vittorio felt his own desire stir and wondered how—and why—he'd kept himself from his wife's bed for so long.

'Where did you go?' he asked, shifting over so she could sit on the bed.

'To the loo.' She gave a little laugh. 'I drank quite a bit of champagne last night. Dutch courage, I suppose.'

'Were you nervous?' He found he was curious to hear what she said, to know what she thought. About everything.

Ana shrugged. 'A bit.' She paused. 'You can't say that our marriage is usual, or normal, and I don't want people…saying things.'

'What kinds of things?'

She gave another shrug, the movement inherently defensive. 'Unkind things.'

Vittorio nodded, realizing for the first time how their marriage bargain might reflect on her, as if she wasn't good enough—or attractive enough—for a proper marriage. For love.

I'm not interested in love.

What he was interested in, Vittorio decided, was

getting his wife into bed as quickly as possible, and then taking his own sweet time in making love to her. Whatever the guests from the party might think, their marriage would certainly be wonderfully normal in at least one respect.

'I know it's Saturday,' Ana said, rising from the bed before Vittorio could even make a move towards her, 'but it was quite cool last night and I wanted to go to the vineyards and check—'

'We have managers for that, Ana.'

She gave a low throaty chuckle that had Vittorio nearly leaping out of bed and dragging her back to it with him. Had she ever laughed like that before? Surely he would have noticed—

'Oh, Vittorio. I don't leave such things to managers. You might, with your million bottles a year—'

'Nine hundred thousand.'

Her eyebrows arched and laughter lurked in her eyes, turning them to silver. 'Oh, pardon me. Well, considering that Viale only has two hundred and fifty—'

'What does it matter?' Vittorio asked, trying not to sound as impatient as he felt. His wife was wearing his shirt and he was half-naked in his own bed; their marriage was still unconsummated nearly a week after the wedding. Why the hell were they talking about wine production?

'It matters to me,' Ana said, a smile still curving that amazingly generous mouth. Vittorio wondered if she knew how she was teasing him. Seducing him.

He'd thought she was insecure, unaware of her own charms, but at the moment his wife looked completely sexy, sensual and as if she knew it. Vittorio felt as if he'd received a very hard blow to the head.

Or to the heart.

Either way, he was reeling.

'It's a beautiful day—' he started again, meaning to end the sentence with *to spend in bed*.

Ana's smile widened. 'Exactly. And I wanted you to show me the Cazlevara vineyards, or at least some of them. It's too nice to be inside.'

Enough, Vittorio thought. Enough talking. He smiled, a sleepy, sensual smile that left no room for Ana to misunderstand. 'Oh, I think we could be inside for a little longer.' Her eyes widened and she hesitated, clearly uncertain. Vittorio extended a hand. 'Come here, Ana.'

'What—' she began and nibbled her lower lip, which was just about the most seductive thing Vittorio had ever seen. He groaned aloud.

'Come *here*.'

She came slowly, hesitantly, perching on the edge of the bed so her shirt rode even higher on her thighs. God give him patience, Vittorio thought, averting his eyes. 'What is it?' she asked, and he heard the uncertainty and even fear in her voice. His wife, Vittorio realized, didn't think he desired her.

He smiled and reached out to brush a strand of silky hair away from her eyes, his fingers skimming the curve of her ear. 'Don't you think,' he murmured, 'we've waited long enough to truly become man and wife?'

Ana's breath hitched. 'Yes, but—'

'But what?'

Again she nibbled her lip. 'You seemed content to wait.'

'Only because I didn't want to hurt you.' Vittorio paused, the moment turning emotional, scaring him. Even now he shied away from the truth of his own feelings. 'I wanted to give you time.'

A smile lurked in Ana's eyes, in the generous curve of her mouth. 'And now you feel you've given me enough time?'

'Oh, yes.' He reached out to stroke her leg; he couldn't help himself, her skin looked so silky. And it felt silky, too. Vittorio suppressed a shudder. 'Do you feel you've had enough time?'

'Oh, yes,' Ana said, and he chuckled at her fervent reply.

'Good.'

Ana sat there in shock, unable to believe Vittorio was saying these things, touching her this way, his fingers skimming and stroking her thigh, sending little shocks of pleasure through her body. His other hand tangled in her hair and he drew her to him, his lips fastening on hers with hungry need; as he kissed her he let out a low groan of relief and satisfaction, and Ana felt another deeper shock: that he seemed so attracted to her, wanted her so, that he couldn't help but touch her, right here in the middle of the morning, in the sunshine, without her having done anything at all. She'd meant to seduce him, to wear a sexy nightdress and have champagne—but this was so much better. So much more real.

'Ana...' Vittorio murmured, his lips now on her ear, her jaw, her neck, 'Ana, you're going on about grapes and vineyards and all I can think about is... this...'

And then it was all Ana could think about too, for Vittorio claimed her lips in a kiss so consuming, so fulfilling, she felt replete and satisfied—as if this kiss could actually be enough—instead of the endless craving she normally felt when they touched.

Vittorio pulled away, just a little bit, but it was enough to make Ana realize that actually she wasn't satisfied at all. She wanted more...and more...and oh, please, a little more than that.

She must have made her need and frustration known, for he chuckled and traced a circle on her tummy with his tongue, making Ana moan aloud, the sound utterly foreign to her. She could hardly believe she was making these sounds, feeling these things.

So *much*.

Vittorio's mouth hovered over her skin. 'I'm going to take my time,' he promised her, and then did just that, while Ana closed her eyes in both surprise and pleasure.

Yet Ana wasn't willing to be a passive recipient, as wonderful as it was. As Vittorio teased her with his mouth and hands, she finally could take no more and flipped him over on his back, straddling his powerful thighs. Vittorio looked so surprised, she laughed aloud.

'You seem to be wearing too many clothes,' she remarked in a husky murmur, and Vittorio nodded.

'I completely agree.'

'Let's do something about that, then.'

'Absolutely.'

She tugged at his pyjama shirt and bottoms, laughing a little bit as buttons snagged and caught, but soon enough he was naked, and Ana pushed back on her elbow to take in his magnificent body, sleek and powerful, all for her. She ran one hand down the taut muscles of his chest.

'I've been wanting to do that for a while,' she admitted a bit shyly, for now that they were both naked, his arousal hard against her thigh, she felt a little uncertain. A little afraid.

'There's a lot I've been wanting to do,' Vittorio admitted, his voice low and a little ragged. 'And I can't take much more waiting, Ana—' True to his word, Vittorio rolled her onto her back, his hands and lips finding her secret sensitive places once again, until Ana found that waiting was the last thing she could think of doing. The wanting took over.

When he finally entered her, filling her up to the very brim with his own self, and with the knowledge of their bodies, fused, joined as *one*, Ana felt no more than a flicker of pain and then the wonderful, consuming certainty that this was the very heart of their marriage, the very best thing that could have ever happened, that they could have ever shared.

Afterwards, as they lay in the warm glow of the sun, their limbs still entangled, she wondered how she'd lived so long without knowing what sex was about. What love was about. For surely the two were utterly entwined, as entwined as her body was now with Vittorio's. She couldn't imagine loving a man she hadn't felt in her own body, and neither could she imagine sharing this with anyone but a man she loved—and that man was Vittorio.

Vittorio ran his hand down her stomach and across the curve of her hip. 'Ana, if I'd known—' he said softly, and she turned to him.

'Known?'

'Known you were a virgin,' he explained. 'I would have—' he smiled ruefully '—I would have taken *more* time, I suppose.'

'You didn't know I was a virgin?' Ana couldn't keep the amusement from her voice. 'Goodness, Vittorio, I thought it was rather obvious.'

'Obvious to you, perhaps,' Vittorio returned. 'But you mentioned a relationship—a man—'

'It never got that far,' Ana replied. The hurt she usually felt when she remembered Roberto's rejection seemed distant, like an emotion she knew intellectually but had never truly felt. It hardly mattered now.

'I'm sorry he hurt you,' Vittorio murmured.

'It's long past,' Ana told him. She pressed her lips to his shoulder; his skin was warm. 'I've completely forgotten it.' She kissed the hollow of his throat, because now that he was truly hers she just couldn't help herself.

It was several hours later when they finally rose from that bed. Ana was sweetly sore all over, her body awakened in every sinew and sense. 'Now the vineyard,' she said and, still lounging among the pillows, Vittorio threw his head back and laughed.

'The vineyard will always be your first love,' he said, his words giving Ana a tiny pang. She wanted to say, *You're my first love*, but she found she could not. The words stuck in her throat, clogged by fear. Instead, she reached for her clothes.

'Absolutely.'

An hour later Ana followed Vittorio from the estate office to one of Cazlevara's finest vineyards. Since Vittorio owned a much bigger operation than she, he had hectares of vines all over Veneto, but the one closest to the castle—on the original estate—was still reserved for the label's most prized grapes.

The sun beat down hot on her head and her shirt was already sticking to her back as Ana walked between the grape plants in their neatly staked rows. She wished she'd worn a hat, or make-up. Instead, without thinking, she'd donned dusty trousers and an old shapeless button-down shirt, her standard field clothes. Hardly an outfit to impress her husband. And just why did she want to impress him? Ana wondered. The answer was painfully clear. Because she still felt a little uncertain, a little worried.

Because she loved him, and she didn't know if he loved her.

If she'd had any sense, she would have worn one of Feliciana's carefully selected outfits—something sexy and slimming—and asked Vittorio to take her to Venice or Verona, even one of the sleepy little villages nestled in one of the region's valleys, somewhere where they could laugh and chat over antipasti and a jug of wine.

She should not have taken him to his work place and donned her own well-worn work clothes to do it! What had she been thinking? Yet, even as she ranted at herself, Ana knew the answers. She loved the vineyards. She loved the grapes, the earth, the sun. The rich scent of soil and growing things, of life itself.

It was the place she loved most of all, and she'd wanted to share it with Vittorio.

Yet, as perspiration beaded on her brow and her boots became covered in a thin film of dust, she wondered if sharing a meal might have been the better choice. She stopped to touch a vine, its cluster of *Nebbiolo* grapes so perfectly proportioned. The grapes were young, firm and dusky, and this breed wouldn't be harvested until October. She bent to inhale the grapes' scent, closing her eyes in sensual pleasure at the beauty of the day: the wind ruffling her hair, the sun on her face, the earthy aroma all around her.

After a few seconds she opened her eyes, conscious of Vittorio's gaze on her. His expression was inscrutable, save for the faintest flicker of a smile curling his mouth.

'I like the smell,' she said, a bit self-consciously. 'I always did. When I was little, my mother found me curled under the bushes asleep.'

Vittorio had, Ana thought, a very funny look on his face now. Almost as if he were in pain. 'You looked like you were enjoying yourself very much,' he said. His voice sounded strangely strangled.

'It was a safe place for me,' Ana acknowledged. 'And, more than that—a bit of heaven.'

'A bit of heaven,' Vittorio repeated. He was standing surprisingly awkwardly, his hands jammed into the front pockets of his trousers, and his voice still sounded—odd.

'Vittorio?' Ana asked uncertainly. 'Are you all right—?'

'Ana.' He cut her off, smiling now, her name coming out in what sounded like a rush of relief. 'Come here.'

Ana didn't know what he meant. They were standing a foot apart; where was she meant to *go*?

Then Vittorio took his hands out of his pockets and, in one effortless movement, he pulled her towards him and buried his head in her hair, breathing in deeply.

'It's the smell of your hair *I* love,' he murmured. His hand had gone under the heavy mass of her hair to her neck. 'I want you,' Vittorio confessed raggedly, 'so much. Come back to the castle with me. Make love to me, Ana.'

Love. Ana couldn't keep the smile from her voice. 'Again?'

'You think once—or twice—is enough?'

She could hardly believe he wanted her so much. It shook her to her very bones, the heart of herself. 'No, definitely not,' she murmured.

'Come back—'

'No.'

Vittorio's face fell in such a comical manner tha Ana would have laughed if she wasn't half-quivering with her own reawakened desire. 'Not at the castle, Vittorio. Here.'

He stared down at the dusty ground. 'Here?' he repeated dubiously.

'Yes,' Ana said firmly, tugging on his hand, 'here.' Here, where he'd found her desirable—sexy—even in her work clothes and wind-tangled hair. Here, where she'd felt safe and heaven-bound all at once, and wanted to again, in Vittorio's arms. Here, because among the grapes and the soil she was her real self, not the woman who wore fancy dresses and high heels and tried to seduce her husband with tricks she couldn't begin to execute with any skill or ease.

Here.

And Vittorio accepted that—or perhaps he couldn't wait any longer—for he spread his blazer, an expensive silk one that was soon covered in dust—on the ground and then lay Ana on it, her hair fanning out around her in a dark silken wave.

Vittorio touched her almost reverently, a look of awe on his face Ana had never expected to see. To know. The ground was hard and bumpy; pebbles dug into her back and the dust was gritty on her skin, but Ana didn't care. She revelled in it, in this. In him.

Vittorio reached for the buttons of her old shirt. 'I never thought white cotton could be so…inflaming,' he murmured, and bent his head to the flesh he'd exposed.

And, as Ana's hand clutched at his hair, she realized she had no idea that she could *feel* so inflamed, as if the very fires of passion were burning her up, turning her craving to liquid heat.

'Vittorio…'

'We may be lying in a field like some farm hand and his dairymaid,' Vittorio murmured against her skin—somehow, all her clothes had been removed, 'but I'm not going to have you like that, with your skirts rucked up around your waist, over in a few pathetic seconds.'

'No, indeed, since I'm not wearing any clothes.'

And, as he smiled against her skin, Ana found she had no thoughts or words left at all. Later, as they lay entangled in a sleepy haze of satisfaction, she murmured, 'We're going to have the most interesting sunburn.'

'Not if I can help it.' In one fluid movement, Vittorio rose from the dusty ground, Ana in his arms. She squealed; she *never* squealed, and yet somehow that ridiculously girlish sound came out of her mouth. Vittorio grinned. 'Put your clothes on, wife,' he said, depositing her on the ground. 'We have a perfectly good bed at home, and I intend to use it... all day.'

'All day?' Ana repeated, still squealing, and then she hurried to yank her clothes back on.

The next few weeks passed in a haze of happiness Ana had never dreamed or even hoped to feel. Although they never spoke of love, her uncertainty melted away in the light of Vittorio's presence and affection, and she hardly thought they needed to. Why speak of love when their bodies communicated far more eloquently and pleasurably? The days were still taken up with work; Ana found herself smiling at the most ridiculous moments, while signing a form or reading a purchasing order. Sometimes, spontaneously, she even laughed aloud.

Vittorio seemed just as happy. His happiness made her happy; his countenance was light, a smile ready on his lips, those onyx eyes lightened to a pewter grey, glinting with humour and love—surely love, for Ana had little doubt that he loved her.

How could he not, when they spent night after night together, not just in passion but in quiet moments afterwards, talking and touching in a way that melted both her body and heart?

He told her bits of his childhood, the hard memories which she'd guessed at, as well as some of the good times: playing *stecca* with his father, going to Rome on a school trip when he was fifteen and getting outrageously drunk.

'It's fortunate I was not expelled.'

'Why weren't you?'

'I told you, I played the trombone,' he replied with a wicked little smile. 'They needed me in the orchestra.'

And Ana told him things she'd never told anyone else, confessed the dark days after her mother's death.

'My father was overwhelmed with grief. He refused to see me for days—locked himself in her bedroom.'

'It's so hard to believe.' Vittorio let his fingers drift through her hair, along her cheek. 'He is so close to you now.'

'It took work,' Ana replied frankly. 'In fact, a week after she died, he sent me to boarding school—he thought it would be easier. For him, I suppose.' It was good, if still hard, to speak of it; bringing light to the dark memories. 'Those two years were the worst of my life.'

Vittorio pressed his lips against the curve of her shoulder. 'I'm sorry.'

'It doesn't matter now.' And it didn't, because in Vittorio's arms she didn't feel big and mannish and awkward; she felt beautiful and sexy and loved.

Loved.

No, she had no doubt at all that Vittorio loved her, no sense that there was anything but happiness—that bit of heaven—ahead of them, shining and pure, stretching to a limitless horizon.

CHAPTER TEN

Six weeks after their wedding, Vittorio came to see Ana at the Viale offices. She looked up from her desk, smiling in pleased surprise as he appeared in the doorway.

'I didn't expect to see you here,' she said, rising to embrace him. Vittorio kissed her with a distracted air, his face troubled before relaxing into a smile that still didn't reach his eyes.

'I have to go to Brazil again. There has been trouble with some of the merchants there.'

'What kind of trouble?' Ana asked, her smile turning to a frown. Her heart had already sunk a bit at the thought: *Brazil*.

Vittorio gave a little shrug. 'It's not worrisome, but important enough that I should go soothe a few ruffled feathers, murmur encouragement in the right ears.'

'You're good at that,' Ana teased, but Vittorio missed the joke entirely.

'I came here because I am leaving this afternoon,

before you return. If I take the private jet to Rio, I can return within a week.'

'A week!' Disappointment swamped her. It seemed like a horribly long time.

'Yes, this is business,' Vittorio said a bit sharply, and his tone as well as his words were like ice water drenching her spirit. Her happiness.

Business. Was Vittorio actually reminding her that business was what their marriage was all about? *Just* business? Ana swallowed dryly. 'Yes, of course.'

'I'll ring you,' he said, pressing a quick kiss against her cold cheek, and then he was gone.

Ana stood in the middle of the office for a few moments, listening to the sounds around her: Vittorio slamming the front door of the building, the purr of the Porsche's engine starting up again, the murmur of voices from other offices. And, the loudest sound of all, the sick thudding of her own frightened heart.

Had she been deceiving herself these last few weeks? Lost in a haze of happiness, mistaking lust for love? Ana moved back to her desk and sat down hard in her chair, her head falling into her hands. She couldn't believe how unsure she felt, how afraid. Her serene certainty that Vittorio loved her had been swept away by one careless remark.

Clearly she hadn't been so certain after all.

The castle felt lonely and quiet when she returned that evening, its endless rooms lost in shadow. Ana told the cook she'd have something in her room rather than face the elegant dining room alone; Constantia had returned to Milan last week and Bernardo, as he so often was, appeared to be out. She didn't want to see anyone.

Marco, the cook, however, looked surprised. 'Ah, but I've made dinner! For two—it is all prepared.'

'For two?' Ana repeated, hope leaping absurdly inside her. Had Vittorio come back? But of course not; he was halfway to South America by now.

'Yes, Signor Bernardo wishes to dine with you.'

Ana felt a finger of foreboding trail along her spine, then shrugged the shivery sensation away. Whatever had passed between Bernardo and Vittorio was long ago, and didn't concern her. Perhaps getting to know her husband's younger brother would go some way in helping to heal his family's rift. Despite the happiness of the last few weeks, Ana knew Vittorio was still snared by the dark memories of his childhood. She saw it when he didn't think anyone was looking, a moment alone lost in sorrowful thought, the shadow of grief in his eyes.

'All right,' she told Marco. 'Thank you.'

As Ana entered the dining room, the setting rays of the sun sending long golden beams of light across the elegant room, she saw the table set cosily for two at one end and Bernardo standing by the window. He started forward as soon as he saw her.

'Ana! Thank you for joining me.'

'Of course, Bernardo. I am happy to dine with you.' Yet, as he took her hands and pressed his cheek against hers in a brotherly embrace, Ana couldn't shake the feeling that Bernardo had an agenda for this meal.

She stepped back, surveying him as he moved to the table to pull out her chair. He was a slighter, paler version of Vittorio, still handsome, with the same dark hair and eyes, yet he lacked his brother's strength and vitality. If they stood next to each other, there could be no doubt as to who was the more dynamic, charismatic and frankly attractive brother. How could Bernardo fail to be jealous?

'Thank you,' she murmured, and sat in the chair Bernardo had drawn for her. He sat opposite and reached for the bottle of red he'd left breathing on a side table.

'One of the vineyard's own?' Ana asked as she watched the rich ruby liquid being poured into her glass.

'In a way. I've been experimenting a bit with mixed grapes.' His expression turned wary, guarded. 'Vittorio doesn't know.'

Ana took a sip of wine. 'But this is delicious.' It was rich and velvety, with a hidden aroma of fruit and spice. She set the glass down and gave Bernardo a frank look. 'Why doesn't Vittorio know you've been experimenting with hybrids? Especially as the result is so pleasing.'

Bernardo gave her a faint smile and took a sip from his own glass. 'Surely you've seen by now that Vittorio and I…' He paused, cocking his head thoughtfully. 'We are not like normal brothers.'

'Of course I've noticed that,' Ana returned. 'In fact,' she added, a bit sharply, 'I even wondered if he would want us to dine like this together, alone.'

'He wouldn't. Not because he thinks it is inappropriate, but because he is afraid I will whisper poison in your ear.'

Ana gestured to her glass. 'Is this poison?' She asked the question lightly, yet Benardo regarded her with grave eyes.

'It is, as far as Vittorio is concerned. He is not interested in anything I have to do with Cazlevara Wines.'

Ana felt a stab of pity. 'Why? Is it simply because of what happened so long ago, when your father died?' Bernardo looked surprised and Ana said quickly, 'I know Constantia tried to take his inheritance, and make you Count. Vittorio told me. Yet that happened so long ago, and you were only a boy—'

'That was merely the beginning,' Bernardo replied. 'I suppose he told you what our childhood was like? We were forced to take sides, Vittorio and I. At first we resisted it. We resented our parents drawing us into their battles. But after time…' He shrugged and spread his hands. 'I admit, I was not a sensible boy. My mother's attention went to my head. When she so clearly preferred me to Vittorio—and my own father did not have so much as a glance for me— well, I flaunted it. I rubbed Vittorio's nose in it. Special presents, trips…these things turn a boy's head. They turned mine.' His mouth twisted in a bitter smile of regret. 'Vittorio saw it all, and said nothing. That only made me angrier. He had my papà's attention and praise, all of it, and I wanted to make him jealous.'

'And of course he was,' Ana cut in. 'Nothing can take the place of a mother's love.'

'Or a father's. I don't know which of us got the better bargain. Vittorio was my father's favourite, but he didn't get spoiled and cosseted like I did. He was whipped into shape.' He held up a hand. 'Not literally. But my father was a hard taskmaster. I remember one time he called Vittorio out of bed—he must have been ten or so, home from boarding school. I was but six at the time. It wasn't even dawn, but my father saw that Vittorio had done poorly on a maths exam. He sat him down at the dining room table and made him write the exam all over again. He didn't stop until every problem was correct. Vittorio worked for hours. He didn't even have breakfast.' Bernardo made a face. 'I remember because I smacked my lips and slurped my juice and he didn't even look up, though he must have been hungry.' Bernardo shook his head, his mouth twisting in a grimace. 'I am not proud of how I behaved over the years, Ana. I freely admit that.'

Ana let out a sorrowful little sigh. It was such a sad, pointless story. Why had Constantia rejected Vittorio so utterly? Couldn't she see how her behaviour had affected him, how her love could have softened her husband's harsh treatment? She'd been so blinded by her own misery, Ana supposed. Arturo's lack of love for his wife had been the rotten seed of it all.

The food had been served, but she found she had no appetite. 'And when your father died? What happened then?'

Bernardo steepled his fingers under his chin. 'By that time the lines were well and truly drawn. Vittorio hated both my mother and me, or at least acted as if he did. He was only fourteen, and he had not one word of kindness for either of us. Oh, he was polite enough, icily respectful, and it drove my mother mad. I suppose Vittorio was so like our father—and my father had never had a true moment of empathy or love for my mother. He was polite, courteous, solicitous even, but there was no love behind it. He was a cold man.'

'Even so, why did your mother try to have the will overturned and disinherit Vittorio? Simply because you were her favourite?' Ana heard the accusation in her own voice. What could justify such cruel, callous behaviour?

Bernardo shrugged. 'Who knows? She has told me she did it because she thought if Vittorio became Count, he would be too hard a man, like my father was. She said she could not bear to see Vittorio become like Arturo.' He smiled sadly. 'I rather thought she believed she was saving him—from himself.'

Ana raised her eyebrows. 'He certainly didn't view it that way.'

'It made things worse, of course,' Bernardo agreed. 'The plan failed, and Vittorio's enmity was cemented. Over the years we have had nothing to say to one another and—' he paused, his gaze sliding from hers '—I have not always acted in a way I could be proud of.' He turned back to face her resolutely. 'And so it continues even now, as you've undoubtedly seen. Which is why I am here.'

Ana met his gaze levelly. 'You have something to ask me.'

'Yes.' Bernardo took a breath and gestured to the wine he'd poured, glinting in their crystal goblets. 'You have tasted my own vintage, Ana, and as an experienced vintner you know it is good. Vittorio is determined never to let me have any control or authority in Cazlevara Wines. God knows, I can understand it. I have not proven myself worthy. I have done things I regret, even as a grown man. But I cannot live like this, under my brother's thumb. Everything is a grudging favour from him. It wears me down to nothing. And to know he would never market this vintage simply because it is mine—'

'Surely Vittorio wouldn't be so unreasonable,' Ana interjected. 'He is a man of business, after all.' How well she knew it.

'When it comes to me and my mother, he is blind,' Bernardo stated flatly. 'Blind and bitter, and I can hardly blame him.'

'So what are you asking of me?'

'You've done some experimenting with hybrids, yes?'

'A little—'

'If you passed this wine off as your own creation, he would accept it.'

'And I would take the credit?'

Bernardo lifted one shoulder in a tiny shrug. 'That does not matter so much to me. It cannot.'

Ana stared at Vittorio's brother, saw the weary resignation on his pale face. She had no doubt that he'd been petted and spoiled as a child, and he'd made his brother's life miserable—more miserable than it already was—well into young adulthood. Yet now she saw a man who was over thirty and resigned never to prove himself, never to have the satisfaction of excelling in a job he was created to do. The injustice and sorrow of it twisted her heart.

'I will not take credit for your own hard work, Bernardo.' He nodded slowly, accepting, his mouth pulled downwards. 'This wine is excellent, and you deserve to be known as its creator.' Ana took a breath. 'So you can either market it under the Viale label or, as I'm sure would be much more satisfying, under the Cazlevara one. This bitter feud between you and Vittorio must end. Perhaps, if he sees how well you have done, he will be convinced.'

Bernardo leaned forward. 'What do you suggest?'

'Why don't you prepare to market the vintage?

Vittorio has given me authority over the vineyards while he is gone.' Ana knew her authority was more perfunctory than anything else; he hardly expected her to change things, or implement strategies such as the one she was suggesting. 'I can arrange a meeting with some merchants in Milan. Start there, and see what happens. By the time Vittorio comes home, God willing, you will have something to show him.' And, Ana added silently, God willing, Vittorio wouldn't be too angry with her. God willing, this feud would finally end and their marriage could continue, grow, work. If he loved her—and she was desperate now to believe he did—his anger would not rule the day.

His love would.

Hope had lit Bernardo's eyes, erasing the resigned lines from his face. He looked younger, happier already. 'What you are doing is dangerous, Ana. Vittorio might be furious. In fact, I know he will be.'

'This feud must end,' Ana said firmly. 'It is the only way forward for any of us. I am not biased by childhood slights the way he is. And I'm sure,' she added with more confidence than she felt, 'my husband will see reason once I have spoken to him.'

It had been a long, hard week, courting the South American merchants. They wanted to rely on their own wines; they were dubious of a European import. Yet, finally, with honeyed words and persuasive arguments, meetings and dinners and tastings, Vittorio had convinced them.

Now he was home and eager—desperate—to see Ana. As his limo pulled up to the castle, Vittorio nearly laughed at himself. He was acting like a besotted boy. He *was* besotted, utterly in love with his wife, and it had taken a week apart to realize just what he was feeling.

Love.

He loved Ana, and he'd felt it in every agonising second he'd spent apart from her, when he'd kept looking for her, even though he knew she was thousands of miles away. He'd felt it when he'd reached for her at night, and both his body and heart had ached when his arms remained empty. It didn't even surprise him, this new-found love; it simply felt too right. He felt completed, whole, and he hadn't realized how much he'd been missing—in and of himself—until he knew that sense of fulfilment, of rightness, caused by loving Ana.

He knew she loved him. He knew it, he'd seen it in her eyes and felt it in her body, yet it still filled him with wonder and incredulous joy. How could he have been so blind to think he didn't want this, didn't need it? Now he could not imagine life without it, without Ana. The very thought left him cold and despairing. But now he didn't despair; now he felt hope. Wonderful, miraculous hope. And he couldn't wait to tell Ana.

The castle was quiet as he entered; it was four

o'clock in the afternoon and he had no doubt Ana
was at her own office. He thought of surprising her
there; he'd make love to her right on her own desk.
His mouth widened into a grin at the thought of it.
First, he would check in at the Cazlevara office and
then…Ana. He could hardly wait.

He was just sorting through the post left by his
secretary when his vineyard manager knocked on
the door.

Vittorio barely glanced up. 'Yes, Antonio?
Everything went well while I was gone?' He tossed
another letter aside, only to pause when he realized
his manager had not spoken. He glanced up, saw the
man twisting his hands together, looking uncertain.
Afraid, even. Vittorio's eyes narrowed. 'Antonio?
Has something happened?'

'It's Bernardo, Lord Ralfino…Bernardo and the
Contessa.'

Vittorio stilled. He felt as if his blood had turned
to ice water; the sense of coldness gave him a chilling
clarity, a freezing resolve. He'd been expecting this,
he realized. He wasn't surprised. 'Has my mother
been plotting again?' he asked levelly. 'Now that I
am married, she seeks to disinherit and discredit me
once more?'

Antonio shook his head, looking wretched. 'Not
the Dowager Contessa, my lord. Your wife.'

For a moment Vittorio couldn't speak. Couldn't
think. The words made no sense. What his manager
was saying was impossible, ridiculous—

Vittorio drew a breath. 'Are you saying my wife is acting with Bernardo?'

'She told me not to ring you,' Antonio confessed unhappily.

'What?' Vittorio could barely process it. His wife had been attempting to deceive him? To scheme against him? The shock left him senseless, reeling, nearly gasping in pain.

'I know you do not wish Bernardo to—well, I knew you'd want this approved,' Antonio continued, 'but since she said—and you'd given her authority—'

Vittorio laid one hand flat on his desk, bracing himself. He would not jump to conclusions. He would *not*. He kept the rage and fear down, suppressing it, even though it fermented and bubbled, threatened to boil over and burn them all. He would not let it. He would listen to Antonio, he would hear Ana's side of the story. He would be fair. 'What has happened, Antonio?'

'Bernardo went to Milan,' the manager confessed. 'He is marketing his own label. I didn't know of it until yesterday, but the Contessa approved it, arranged the meeting—'

'His own label?' Vittorio repeated blankly. Was his brother actually trying to take over the family winery, to make it his own? And Ana was *helping* him? Had they been planning this—this *takeover*—together while he was gone? Or even before? He could hardly make sense of it, his heart cried out its innate, desperate rejection of such lies, even as his mind coolly reminded him that this was exactly how he'd felt returning from his father's funeral, hoping—desperately hoping—that now his father was dead his mother might turn to him, if not with open arms, then at least with a smile.

She'd turned her back instead. Something had died in Vittorio then, that last frail hope he'd never realized he'd still clung to. The desire for love. The hope it would find him. He'd lost it then, or thought he had, only to find the desire and the hope—the need for love—inside him, latent, and with Ana it had begun to grow, young and fragile, seeking her healing light.

Now he felt as if it had been felled at its tender root. His heart had become a barren wasteland, frozen and unyielding. He turned back to Antonio. 'Thank you for telling me. I will deal with it now.'

'I would have rung you, but since the Contessa was meant to be in charge—'

'I completely understand. Do not think of it again.' Vittorio dismissed the man with a nod, then turned to stare blindly out of the window. Rows upon rows of neat growing grapes stretched to the horizon, Cazlevara's fortune, his family's life blood. He'd made love to Ana out there, among those vines. He'd held in her arms and loved her.

Loved her.

And now she'd betrayed him. He tried to stay reasonable, to keep the anger and hurt and oh, yes, the fear from consuming him, but they rose up in a red tide of feeling until he couldn't think any more. He could only feel.

He felt the hurt and the pain and the sorrow, the *agony* of his mother and brother's rejection, over and over again. Day after day of trying to please his father, only to strive more and more; nothing he'd ever done was enough. And then when his father had died, torn between despair and relief, he'd wanted to turn to his mother, thinking that now she would accept him, love him even, only to realize she'd rejected him utterly.

And now. This. Ana had somehow been working against him with his brother, waiting until he was gone to use the authority he'd given her on *trust* to discredit him. This, he acknowledged, was the worst betrayal of all.

'Lord Cazlevara is here to see you, Signorina Vi—Lady Cazlevara.'

Ana half-rose from the desk, smiling at Edoardo. 'You don't need to stand on ceremony, Edoardo. Send him in!' Yet, even as a smile of hope and welcome—how she'd missed him!—was spreading across her face, another part of Ana was registering the look of wariness on her assistant's face and wondering why he seemed so uncomfortable.

'Good afternoon, Ana.'

'Vittorio!' The word burst from Ana's lips and, despite his rather chilly greeting, she couldn't keep from smiling, from walking towards him, her arms outstretched, needing his touch, his kiss—

Vittorio didn't move. Ana dropped her arms, realization settling coldly inside her. He'd heard about Bernardo, obviously. He knew what she'd done. And he hadn't liked it.

'You're angry,' she stated, and Vittorio arched one eyebrow.

'Angry? No. Curious, perhaps.' He spoke with arctic politeness that froze Ana's insides. She hadn't heard that voice in such a long time; she'd forgotten just how cold it was. How cold it made her feel. Vittorio leaned against the door frame, hands in his pockets, and waited.

Ana took a breath. She'd been preparing for this conversation, had known that Vittorio, on some level, would not be pleased. He'd try to distance himself; that was how he stayed safe. She *knew* that, yet she'd trusted what she felt for him—and what she believed and hoped he felt for her—that their love would make him see reason. She'd told herself so hundreds of times over the last week, yet now that the time had come and Vittorio was standing here looking so icy and indifferent, all the calm explanations she'd come up with seemed to have vanished, leaving her with nothing but a growing sense of panic, a swamping fear. She didn't want her husband looking at her this way, talking to her as if she were a stranger he didn't really like. She couldn't bear it. 'Vittorio,' she finally said, and heard the plea in her voice even though her words sounded firm, 'Bernardo showed me the vintage he's created. He's been working with hybrids—you didn't know—'

'Funny, I thought I knew everything that happened in my company. And, as I recollect, my brother was assistant manager, not head vintner. Or did you give him a promotion in my absence?' He spoke pleasantly, yet Ana heard and felt the terrible coldness underneath. It crept into her bones and wound its icy way around her heart. She felt like shivering, shuddering, crying out.

This was what Constantia had lived with day in, day out. This was what Vittorio had been to her, a man who refused to be reached, whose heart was enclosed in walls of ice. No wonder the woman had gone half-mad. She already felt perilously close to the edge of reason after just a few minutes under his freezing stare.

'No, I didn't give him a promotion,' Ana replied as levelly as she could. 'I wouldn't presume to do such a thing—'

'Wouldn't you?'

Ana forced herself to ignore the sneering question. 'But I did allow him to market his own wine. He's in Milan right now, talking to some merchants about it. I thought we could put it in the catalogue this autumn—'

'Oh, you did, did you?' Vittorio took a step into the room, his pleasant mask dropped so Ana saw the icy rage underneath. 'You didn't waste much time, did you, Ana?' he asked, fairly spitting the words. 'The moment I'd gone, you were plotting and planning behind my back.'

Ana quelled beneath the verbal attack. Did he think so little of her? 'It wasn't a plot, Vittorio,' she insisted, 'though I can understand why you might think that way. But I am not your mother, and Bernardo has changed—'

Vittorio gave a sharp laugh. 'Nothing has changed. Don't you think I have a reason for keeping him on as short a leash as I do?'

Ana struggled to keep her calm. 'Vittorio, your brother was ten when your mother tried to disinherit you—'

'And he was twenty when he tried to sabotage the winery and discredit me to my customers, and twenty-five when he embezzled a hundred thousand euros. Don't you think I know my own brother?'

Ana stared at him in shock, her mouth dropping open before she had the sense to snap it shut. Realization trickled icily though her. 'I didn't know those things,' she finally said quietly. Vittorio gave another disbelieving laugh and she thought of Bernardo's words: *I have done things I regret, even as a grown man.* She almost felt like laughing hysterically, despite the panic and the fear. Perhaps she should have asked Bernardo to clarify what he'd meant. Perhaps she shouldn't have leapt in so rashly, thinking she could heal old wounds, hurts that had never scarred over, just festered and bled—

Still, Ana knew there was more going on here, more at risk than Vittorio's sour relationship with his brother. There was his relationship with *her*, a fundamental issue of trust and love. She had to ask crucial questions, and now she was afraid of their answers.

'I really didn't know everything he'd done,' she said, trying to keep her voice steady. 'Still, I believe Bernardo has changed. If you just give him a chance—'

'So he's convinced you,' Vittorio stated quietly. He turned away so she couldn't see his face. 'He's turned you from me.'

Ana suddenly felt near to tears. Vittorio's voice sounded so final, so *sad*. 'Vittorio, it's not like that! I just wanted to give Bernardo a chance, not only for his sake, but for *ours*.'

'*Ours*,' Vittorio repeated, the word dripping sarcasm.

'Yes, ours, because your hatred of him poisons everything! Poisons—' She stopped, not wanting to expose herself so utterly and admit she loved him. 'And he could be a credit to you,' she continued quietly. 'He rang me from Milan this morning, and the meetings went well. He's not trying to take some kind of control—'

'So he says.'

'This bitterness must end,' Ana stated. Her voice trembled and she forced herself to go on, to say the words she'd shied away from. The truth was the only thing that had the power to heal. 'It poisons you, and it poisons our love.'

She felt as if she'd laid down a live wire; the room crackled with uncontained energy. *Love*. She'd said it, admitted to that most dangerous forbidden feeling.

Vittorio turned around; his eyes were like two pools of black ice. 'Love?' he enquired silkily. 'What are you talking about, Ana?'

Ana blinked, forcing back the tears. She would be strong now, even if that strength meant being more vulnerable than she ever had before. 'I love you, Vittorio. I gave Bernardo a chance for love of you—'

'Just like my mother took my inheritance, claiming she did it out of love for me?' Vittorio mocked.

'Is that what she said?'

'Or something like it. I found it rather hard to believe.'

Yet Ana didn't. She could see Constantia's twisted reasoning now, understand how she might do anything—*anything*—to keep Vittorio from becoming the cold, hard man his father had been, and had wanted to make him. Yet, right now before her eyes, he was changing, hardening, the last weeks of love and gentleness falling away as if they'd never been, leaving her with a man she didn't like or even know.

'It's true, Vittorio. I don't doubt Bernardo has hurt you, as has Constantia, but this cannot go on. You are all poisoned by it—all three of you. I thought if

Bernardo proved himself to you, you could see each other as equals. Forgive each other and learn to—'

'Oh, Ana, this is all sounding very cosy,' Vittorio drawled. 'And completely unrealistic. I didn't marry you to play therapist to my family. I married you to be loyal to *me*.'

Ana blinked. 'And does that loyalty mean blind obedience? I can't take any decisions for myself? You didn't want a lapdog, you said. You rather touchingly referred to our marriage as one of *partnership*—'

'A business partnership,' Vittorio corrected. 'That is what I meant.'

Ana swallowed, struggling to stay reasonable, as if her heart and soul hadn't been shredded to pathetic pieces as they spoke. 'Yet you do not want me to have any concern with your business—'

'I do not want you to use your influence to put my brother's concerns forward!' Vittorio cut her off, his voice rising to a near-shout before he lowered it again to no more than a dark whisper. 'You have betrayed me, Ana.'

'I love you,' Ana returned. Her voice shook; so did her body. 'Vittorio, I *love* you—'

He shook his head in flat dismissal. 'That wasn't part of our bargain.'

She searched his face, looking for any trace of compassion or even regret. Every line, every angle was hard and implacable. He had become a stranger, a terrible stranger. 'I know it wasn't,' she said quietly. 'But I fell in love with you anyway, with the man you...you seemed to be. Yet now—' she took a breath '—you are so cold to me. Vittorio, do you not love me at all?'

A muscle jerked in Vittorio's cheek and he didn't answer. He gazed down at her, his eyes hard and unrelenting, and suddenly Ana could stand it no more. She'd felt this exposed only once before in her life, when she'd flung herself at Roberto, hoping he would take her into his arms and admit he was attracted to her, to make his love physical as well as emotional. She'd been rejected then, utterly, or so she'd thought. Yet that moment was nothing—*nothing*—compared to this. Now Vittorio was rejecting her emotionally; he was rejecting her heart rather than her body and it hurt so much more.

It hurt unbearably.

'I see you don't,' she said quietly and, when Vittorio still didn't answer, Ana did the only thing she could think of doing, the only option left to her. She fled.

In a numb state of grief—the same kind of frozen despair she'd felt when her mother had died—Ana walked away from her office. She didn't think about where she was going until she found herself on the dirt road back to Villa Rosso, its mellow stone and terracotta tiles gleaming in the afternoon sun.

She was going home.

The villa was quiet when she entered, her footsteps falling softly on the tiled floor of the foyer. She

headed for the stairs but heard her father's voice call
out from his study.

'Hello? Is someone there?'

'It's me, Papà.' Ana paused on the stairs; her father
came to the hall. He took one look at her face—Ana
could only imagine how terrible she looked—and
gasped aloud.

'Ana! What has happened?'

Ana gave a sad little smile. She felt as if her whole
body were breaking, her soul rent into pieces. 'I discovered you were right, Papà. Love isn't very comfortable, after all.'

Enrico's face twisted in sorrow, but Ana knew
she could not bear even his sympathy now. She just
shook her head and walked with heavy steps upstairs, to the room she had not slept in since she'd
got married.

Married. Vittorio was her husband, yet she hardly
knew what that meant any more.

She spent the night alone, lying on her bed, watching the moon rise and then descend once more. She
didn't sleep. She found herself reliving the joy of
the last few weeks, now made all the sweeter by its
brevity. Vittorio kissing her, taking her in his arms.
Laughing as they played *stecca* again; he'd won that
time. Talking about the vineyards, and grapes, and
wine, gesturing with their hands, shared enthusiasm
in their voices. The way he touched her casually, a
hand on hers, when they were reading in bed, simply
because he wanted to feel her next to him. And then

later, the way he touched her so her body cried out in pleasure. So many memories, so many wonderful, sweet, *terrible* memories, because she was afraid they were all she'd ever have.

Was their marriage actually over? She could hardly believe he had rejected her so utterly; she thought of trying to see him again and then knew she couldn't. She couldn't face that hard, blank face again. She couldn't face the feeling of being so raw, so exposed and rejected again. Not by Vittorio, not by the man—the only man—she'd ever love.

She pressed her face into her pillow and willed the tears to come; crying would bring relief of a sort. They didn't. Some things, Ana knew, were too deep for tears.

Enrico knocked on her door in the morning, begging her to take a bit of breakfast. 'Ana, have some toast at least,' he called, his voice sounding thin and frail. 'I told the cook not to make kippers. I know they put you off.'

Ana couldn't even summon a smile. 'Don't trouble yourself, Papà. I'm not hungry. I just need to be alone for a little while.'

She needed to be alone to grieve the ending of her marriage, for surely that was what this was. Vittorio had not come to see her and Ana dreaded some horrible letter, a cold official ending to their marriage. Although, she reminded herself, he'd said divorce was not an option.

Yet the alternative—the cold convenient marriage

she'd once agreed to—would be so much worse, for affection and respect had been obliterated. All that was left was duty.

Funny, Ana thought distantly as she lay on her bed, watching the sun rise in the sky, still in her clothes from the day before, how she had once convinced herself she could accept such a thing. A loveless marriage, a business arrangement. She'd deceived herself. Love wasn't comfortable but it was everything.

In the early evening, Enrico knocked again. *'Dolcezza—'*

'I'm still not hungry,' Ana called.

'You don't need to eat,' her father called back, 'but your husband is here, and he wants to see you.'

Ana stilled. Her hands clenched into fists on her bed covers. 'I can't see him, Papà,' she said, her voice no more than a choked whisper.

'Please, Ana. He is desperate for you.'

'Desperate?' She said the word disbelievingly, yet still laced with damning hope.

'Desperate, *rondinella*.' Vittorio's voice, no more than a husky whisper, made Ana freeze. Distantly, she heard her father's footsteps patter down the hall and, after a moment, her heart beating with hard, heavy thuds, she went to open the door. Vittorio stood there, ushaven, his hair rumpled, still wearing his clothes from yesterday. His eyes remained grave as he gave her a small uncertain smile.

'You look as awful as I do,' Ana said.

Vittorio touched her cheek. 'You have not been crying, at least.' His own eyes looked red.

'Some things are too deep for tears,' Ana told him and he stepped into the room. She leaned against the door, her arms crossed, unwilling to relax her guard. Afraid to hope.

'Oh, Ana.' Vittorio shook his head, his voice choking a little bit. 'I made you so unhappy.'

'Yes, you did,' Ana agreed, and was amazed at how level her voice sounded, as if she wasn't affected at all. As if she wasn't dying inside.

'I was so angry,' Vittorio said quietly. 'And it blinded me. All I could see—feel—was betrayal.'

'I know.'

His smile was touched with sorrow. 'It's not an excuse, is it?'

'No.'

'Just a reason.' He sighed again. 'I have a lot to learn, I suppose, if you will consent to be my teacher.'

Ana shook her head. 'I don't want to be your teacher, Vittorio. I want to be your wife. And that means you need to trust me.'

'I know,' Vittorio said in a low voice. 'I know I should have, but I couldn't *think*—'

'It doesn't even matter.' Ana cut him off, her voice tight. 'I realize the bargain we made doesn't work for me, Vittorio. I can't…I can't accept our marriage on your terms.'

'What?' He looked shocked. 'What are you talking about?'

She swallowed, her voice raw. 'I need more from you than your trust. I need your love.'

He stared at her, slack-jawed, and Ana braced herself for his refusal. His rejection. It never came.

'I do love you, Ana,' Vittorio said, his voice a throb of intensity. 'And it has terrified me. That's why I acted like I did yesterday. Not another excuse—just the truth. I am sorry. So sorry. Please forgive me.'

Ana could hardly believe what he'd said. 'You love me?' she repeated, and he offered her a tremulous smile.

'Utterly. Unbearably. I spent the most wretched night last night, and for love of you—I thought I'd just gone and thrown out the most wonderful thing that's ever happened to me, and for what? My own pride?'

She shook her head. Hope bubbled up inside her, an everlasting well of joy. 'I shouldn't have acted without you, but I thought…I thought to help heal the past—'

'And you have,' Vittorio said. 'Already, it has begun. When you walked out of that office I realized you might actually be walking away from me for ever, and I was letting you go. I was devastated, in agony, and I knew I could not let my pride keep you from me. I spoke to Bernardo, and to my mother.' He took a breath, offering her a wry smile. 'It was not easy or comfortable for any of us. We have all committed wrongs against each other and there is still much to do, to say and to forgive. Yet we have begun. You have helped us, Ana. You are the best thing to have come into my life.'

Ana's throat ached with unshed tears and suppressed emotion. 'And you are the best thing in mine.' Still, she felt the fear lurking in the dark corners of her heart. It seemed so hard to believe, too wonderful to be true. To last. 'Yesterday you were so cold, so hard to me—'

Vittorio reached for her fingers and pressed them against his lips. 'I do not want to be a hard man,' he confessed, his voice a ragged whisper, his eyes glinting with unshed tears of his own. 'God knows, I don't. Yet, when I am afraid, I find that is how I become, for it is what I learned as a boy.'

'I know it is,' Ana whispered, remembering what both Constantia and Bernardo had told her. They'd helped her understand Vittorio, and she was grateful to them for that.

'It is no excuse,' Vittorio replied resolutely. 'And yet you have changed me, Ana. I am so grateful for that. I realized just how much you've changed me when you left me yesterday. I do not want to be that man any more. With you, I am not him.'

He touched her cheek, resting his forehead against hers. 'Can you forgive me, *rondinella*, for those moments when I became him again? Can you forgive me, and believe in the man I am trying to become?'

Ana thought of the man who had comforted her as a grieving child so many years ago; she remembered his many kindnesses over the last few months. She recalled the wonder and joy she'd felt in his arms. 'You are that man, Vittorio. You always have been.'

He kissed her then sweetly, so very sweetly, a kiss that was healing and hope together. 'Only because of you, Ana. Only because of you.'

She laughed, a tremulous, muffled sound, for the knowledge that Vittorio loved her—that this was *real*—was too wonderful, too overwhelming. She trusted it now; she believed in it, and it was good.

It was amazing.

Vittorio touched her cheek; it came away damp. 'It's all right to cry, *rondinella*,' he whispered and Ana laughed again, entwining his fingers with her own as she kissed him once more.

'For joy,' she said. 'This time for joy.'